WARLORD'S BABY

WARLORD BRIDES

NANCEY CUMMINGS
STARR HUNTRESS

MENURA PRESS

COPYRIGHT

Warlord's Baby: Warlord Brides

Warriors of Sangrin 5

Copyright Nancey Cummings

Cover design by Nancey Cummings

Published July 2017

Published by Menura Press

Author's Note: This is a work of fiction and all people, places and incidents are products of the author's imagination. All characters depicted in this work of fiction are eighteen years of age or older.

INTRODUCTION

The Story So Far

When aliens arrived on Earth, it happened with an invasion—just like the sci-fi movies taught us to expect.

The vicious Suhlik meant to enslave Earth and rob her of her resources. Only the Mahdfel warriors were able to stand against them.

Once the slaves of the Suhlik, the Mahdfel won their freedom. But as a lingering reminder of their oppression at the hands of the Suhlik they are unable to have female children.

Now, in exchange for the protection of Earth, the hunky alien warriors demand only one price: Every childless, single and otherwise healthy woman on Earth is tested for genetic compatibility for marriage with a Mahdfel warrior. If the match is 98.5% or better, the bride is instantly teleported away to her new mate.

No exceptions.

A year ago Mercy was matched to Paax Nawk, a warrior who had no interest in taking a mate. When the previous warlord threatened her life, Paax challenged the male and won, becoming the new warlord.

Now they await their first child.

CHAPTER 1

Mercy

M ercy glowed in the dark.

No one really told her what to expect when she was expecting an alien's baby.

The same genetic quirk that allowed her husband's tattoos to glow caused the amniotic fluid to glow. Between her unborn son punching her bladder, the constant ache in her back, swollen feet, sensitive nipples and the mood swings from teary-eyed sentimental mush to full-on grumpy-pants, Mercy was ready to get this kid out of her.

Don't get her wrong. She loved being pregnant. She loved feeling the baby inside her move and she loved the look of pure joy in her husband's eyes when the baby kicked. Even with all that, she was tired and uncomfortable and ready to hold her baby in her arms.

Soon.

How soon, exactly? No one would say. Medic Kalen was oddly tight lipped about the subject and his wife, Meridan, just nodded with a comforting smile, saying the baby needed a "little more time in the oven."

Easy for her to say, she wasn't hauling the *oven* all over creation.

Mercy rubbed ineffectively at the back of her neck. If she could just get a good night's sleep her mood would improve. At the moment, everything irritated her. The lighting was too harsh and hurt her eyes. The battle cruiser smelled. Not bad, just stale like the air filters needed to be changed. In an effort to placate his wife, Paax had his warriors running all over the ship replacing them, but installing new filters did nothing. And sounds drove her crazy. The background hum of the ship was too loud.

Mercy would lay on her side in bed, pillow at her back, wedged between her knees and at her stomach, listening to Paax breathe. He didn't snore, just breathed. It never bothered her before but now it was too loud. She wanted complete silence to sleep but how could she complain that her husband *breathed* too loudly? At least she recognized her unreasonableness for the pregnancy induced crazy that it was. That counted for something, right?

What she wouldn't give for a solid night's sleep. Or even a good nap.

Focusing on the negative wouldn't improve the situation.

Mercy took a calming breath, counted backwards from ten, and exhaled. The meditation garden quickly became her favorite place on the *Judgment*.

Water from the streaming fountain arch splashed on pebbles. Cushions propped up behind her back supported her in the large papasan chair. The air was cool and fresh. Bird song played from cleverly hidden speakers.

As large as a small city, when she arrived a year ago the battle cruise was… stark. Bare bones and utilitarian. The previous warlord had stripped the *Judgment* of anything that reminded him of his deceased mate, including the mates of other warriors. All females, and their mates, were removed. With the female population gone, the warlord saw little need for luxuries like greenery or social spaces, fresh food or entertainment. Endless training and prepackaged rations were good enough.

It was miserable.

Fortunately, her husband, the new warlord, agreed to improve the quality of life on the battle cruiser. Green spaces that served no purpose other than to be green and pleasant returned. A real chef and cooks brought freshly prepared meals to the clan. Social spaces appeared but the Mahdfel had a hard time grasping social events. Battle was hard wired into the alien warriors and the idea of "just relaxing" was anathema to them.

Fortunately, they did understand meditation, in so much as it focused a warrior's mind before battle. Whatever. Mercy didn't have the energy to argue. Paax carved out a meditation garden complete with a fountain, the perfect chair for her aching pregnant back, and even a master gardener to maintain the slice of heaven.

"Warlord's female," a voice said, disturbing her peace, "you are needed in Medical."

Time for her twice daily check up.

Pregnancy was always risky. Pregnant with a Mahdfel baby? Even more so. Pregnant with the warlord's baby? Risky or not, everyone acted as if she were the most fragile, precious thing imaginable.

Mercy was miserable.

Her pregnancy started with bi-weekly checkups. As her belly grew, so did the medical appointments, from once every two weeks to weekly, then twice a week, then once a day. Now, in the final days before her labor, the appointments were twice a day. She might as well have a medic slap a monitor on her and follow her around, like her security detail. What was another purple, horned alien male in her entourage?

"Warlord's female?"

"Is something wrong with her? Why does she not answer?"

"We will call a medic now. I refuse to allow the warlord's female to be injured on my watch."

Mercy held up a hand before Braith, Kleve or Jolyon called down the wrath of Medic Kalen. "I'm fine. Just one more minute. I'm actually comfortable and I don't want to get up."

"Your medical appointments are non-negotiable," Braith said.

"Help me up then," she said, stretching out her arms. Any shyness or shame at needing help up had long since vanished. This was her reality and Braith, Kleve and Jolyon had been her assigned security for the last month. Initially her security detail started with one warrior. As her belly grew, much like with the frequency of medical appointments, her security detail grew. When the baby finally arrived, Mercy imagined another warrior would be added, too.

Mercy took another deep breath, focusing on the positive. Her husband loved her. He was kind and passionate and gave her everything she asked. Paax brought her mother, Dorothy, from Earth and used Mahdfel medicine to heal the old injuries she received during the invasion. Paax didn't have to do that. He didn't have to do any of it: the meditation garden, the cook, the fresh meals, or the slow but steady refurbishing of his battle cruiser, but he did it for her.

Hormones and the sheer uncomfortable nature of being very pregnant made her grumpy. Focus on the positive. She was healthy. The baby was healthy. She loved her husband and he loved her.

The medical bay was like a second home at this point. Kalen kept a human-sized exam table and chair just for her, complete with pillows for her back. She climbed onto the table, ready for Kalen to wave a scanner over her, frown and then insist that everything was "acceptable."

His reactions never felt acceptable. They felt like he kept something back.

"Is Paax here?" Mercy asked, scooting back on the padded table.

"The warlord sends his regrets," Kalen said crisply, eyes fixed on the scanner.

Mercy's smile fell. "Oh. He said he would be here." She didn't want to whine or cry but emotion bubbled up unbidden at the back of her throat. Stupid hormones. She was disappointed, yes, but her body was at the cusp of bawling her eyes out like Paax broke her heart. She could just have easily flown into a rage. Her emotions weren't real but hormone induced. Still, he did promise to be there and what type of husband couldn't keep a promise to his heavily pregnant wife?

The waterworks started and Mercy was helpless to stop them.

Kalen jerked the scanner away, alarmed, and took a step back. "Meridan," he called, the unease in his voice making Mercy cry harder.

She didn't want to cry. She didn't, but she couldn't stop, either.

Meridan came over quickly, hair pulled back and wearing bright pink scrubs. She looked every inch the friendly, compassionate nurse. Tension eased in Mercy's chest as Meridan produced a box of tissues. She was always so thoughtful toward Mercy, and she had the sweetest little girl. And just like that, Mercy grew teary eyed again thinking of Estella stolen away by the Suhlik and rescued by Paax's clan, growing up in a loving family now, complete with a dog. Never mind, that the dog had actually been Mercy's puppy, Cookie. The love between girl and dog was instant and Mercy couldn't separate the two. Besides, she didn't have the energy to give Cookie all the attention and exercise he deserved.

"How is Cookie?" she asked, chest heaving.

"Having the time of his doggy life. Estella keeps feeding him table scraps and she thinks we don't notice. Cookie's gained three pounds."

"I'm glad. They deserve—" Ragged breath. "To be ha-happy—" Mercy broke down into tears again.

"What did you say to her," Meridan snapped at Kalen.

"I did not say anything." The alien medic's back stiffened.

"Baloney. This is not the face of a calm and relaxed woman." Meridan crouched down next to Mercy, eyes level. "Was he rude? Did he make you feel silly for asking a simple question?" Eyes narrowed, she glanced over her shoulder, back toward the medic.

Mercy shook her head. "It's not that," she managed to say between shuddering breathes. She hated this. She hated being a blubbering mess, held hostage by hormones.

"The warlord is unable to attend her check-up," Kalen said.

"Call him," Meridan said immediately.

"I will not."

Mercy scrubbed a tissue at her face, breathing under a thin layer of control. "It's fine. Paax is busy."

Meridan stood and grabbed the scanner out of Kalen's hands. "Honestly, the two of you. Call him. Tell him to get his purple butt down here and provide the emotional support his mate obviously needs."

"I cannot order the—"

"Are you the head of medicine? Is your top priority the well-being of the warlord's mate? I thought the point of all this was to keep her stress levels down. But, please, just stand there and pretend that you don't have the rank to give the warlord a direct order." Meridan didn't pull punches. Mercy liked that about her, also.

Kalen nodded. "Very well."

Meridan's attention returned to Mercy and the scanner in her hands.

"We're not going to get Kalen in trouble, are we?" Mercy asked.

"Nope," she said without hesitation. "I think he relishes any opportunity he gets to give the warlord orders. It's probably not good for his ego, though."

Kalen snorted. He held out his hand for the scanner.

"Well?" Meridan asked, withholding the instrument.

"The warlord is on his way."

"Good," she said, handing it over.

"Your vitals are strong," Kalen said, reading the instrument. "You will have healthy sons soon."

"Sons?" Mercy asked, dumbstruck. No one had ever

mentioned the possibility of multiple babies. Was that why she was so huge? She had twins? Paax was a twin. Those type of things ran in families. Her heart raced with panic.

Twins.

One baby was more than enough. How could she handle twice the diapers, feedings, naps, tantrums and everything else that came with motherhood?

Kalen frowned. "Son. I misspoke."

"Enjoy it," Meridan added quickly. "He doesn't like to make mistakes and hates it when anyone catches them."

"So just one baby?"

"Just one," Meridan said. "Big and healthy."

"Paax told me Mahdfel-Sangrin babies gestate quickly. This is—"

"Nine months almost to the day," she said. "Sangrins have a gestation of seven months. Remember, this baby is half human."

"And he's taking the full nine months." Mercy sighed. "Any idea when I'm going to be due?"

"They've—he's dropped lower in your pelvis," Meridan said, placing a hand on Mercy's stomach to demonstrate. "Do you feel him down there?"

Mercy nodded.

"And your cervix is thinning, which is what we want to see."

"But no time frame?" She could handle a day or two but another week? Two weeks? Didn't Mercy's mother warn her that Mercy herself showed up two weeks overdue as a baby?

"Soon."

Her shoulders slumped. Soon. That tired old routine.

Soon could not come fast enough.

CHAPTER 2

Paax

Paax paced the length of the bridge of the battle cruiser *Judgment*. The short journey took him from the communication station, whose officer was currently trying to explain the very detailed reasons how they lost all contact with Earth, Sangrin and the council, to the science station and back. A solar flare knocked out the communication relays and it would be several hours before the systems were operational.

"It seems to me that a solar flare is something that is easily anticipated and avoided," he said, grinding his teeth. What was the point of a science station if they didn't use science?

"I don't know, sir," Antu said. "You'd have to speak to navigation or the astro lab."

"And why were our shields unable to withstand a solar flare?"

"You'd need to ask engineering."

Paax cocked his head to one side, considering the communications officer. He found no disrespect in his tone, just a crisp, professional indifference, but it seemed like the warrior knew very little about his station and did none of the actual work. "When you say repairs will take several hours, how many hours is several hours?"

"Forty-eight."

Two days?

"Are we waiting for engineering to repair or completely fabricate and replace parts?"

"You'd have to ask—"

Paax held up a hand. "To ask engineering. Good suggestion, Antu. Go down to engineering and apply your expertise to speed along the process."

Antu gave him a blank stare.

Paax held his challenging gaze. He could threaten the male or pummel him into submission but that would make Paax look weak in the eyes of the clan. A warlord commanded the respect and obedience of his clan. He did not threaten or use his physical prowess to demand it. A warlord did not work his way up the ranks. He led because he bested the old warlord in battle and the clan followed him. It was the right of any warrior to challenge the warlord if they thought they could best him. Antu was completely within his right to challenge Paax, even if he was a lazy, insubordinate little shit.

Antu's gaze fell to the floor. "Yes, sir."

Paax watched Antu's receding figure as he scurried off.

That one was trouble, just like his brother, Antomas. While Paax did not have to deal with Antomas on a daily basis, the Sangrin council spoke of the young warlord often enough for Paax to draw an unfavorable opinion. The council's words were of praise but Paax saw nothing but a lunatic berserker who found himself leading a small clan and a nimble ship. Antomas had a growing reputation for daring raids, daring battles and unchecked ambition. The council was concerned that his small ship would not be enough to hold the warlord and he would need a larger ship, perhaps a battle cruiser…

Paax thought he hated politics when his brother served as the warlord. Now limitless loathing filled him.

Paax knew very well the council was enamored of Antomas' rising star and considered Paax too old and too conservative to lead the largest battle cruiser in the fleet, but that was another problem to add to the list. Two days without any communications was far too serious.

While he did not appreciate Antu's insubordinate excuses for why he failed at his post, Antu had a point. He just worked the comm relays. Astro lab, navigation and even engineering failed to alert him about an incoming solar flare, a flare they could have avoided or at least been shielded against.

Someone wanted the *Judgment* to be out of contact and anything could happen in two days.

The clan was restless. Paax knew that. Dissent grew. The pressure for change was internal as well as external. A challenge was coming and his head of security was still on Earth and his mate about to give birth and the battle cruiser was essentially silenced—

The challenge would be soon. Now was the perfect time, whether by happenstance or fabricated, now was the time for a challenger to arise.

He couldn't stop them. Wouldn't stop them. Every warrior had the right to challenge the warlord. Whether it was a good idea or not—that was a different matter. If Paax avoided or deferred the challenge, he would be seen as weak and the challengers would only multiply. When Paax assumed the mantle of warlord, he battled a handful of challengers but he prevailed in the arena. In truth, he knew it was not because of his superior skills. The clan was in shambles at the time and no one wanted the job of rebuilding. However, it was a year later and the clan flourished. The warriors grew restless, perhaps thinking that they could do a better job—

Not for the first time, conflicting emotions of regret and anger rose up as he thought about Omas, the last warlord. He nearly destroyed the clan in his grief at the death of his mate. He put Paax in the terrible situation where he had to defeat the warlord to save not only his life but the life of his mate. Omas had also been crazed, twisted physically and mentally by an experimental treatment Paax developed in a desperate attempt to save the warlord's life.

Omas also forced Paax into accepting a match and taking a mate, when Paax refused for years to take a mate. Mercy was the love of his life. A year ago he had not even met the little Terran female who would claim his heart, and now he couldn't imagine life without her.

Omas was also his twin brother.

His mad, twin brother forced Paax to kill him in battle because that was the only way to save Mercy's life.

Conflicted did not begin to describe the situation. Furious. Remorseful. Thankful. All that applied in equal measure.

"Does anyone else think astro lab or navigation should do their job for them?" Paax asked loudly, eyes scanning the bridge.

No one met his gaze. Good. A challenge would come but not at that moment. He had time to prepare, to devise a strategy. He couldn't avoid the challenge but he could meet it early, catch it on the wrong foot and have the advantage.

It was as good a plan as any. Mylomon, his second in command, would be proud.

"Sir," a voice came over the wrist comm unit. Internal communications seemed to be working just fine.

"Medic, report," Paax said.

"Your mate requires your presence in medical."

"Is she harmed in any way?"

A pause. "She requires you."

Paax sighed. He knew some of the warriors believed he

doted on his mate. He did. Why shouldn't he? The two main impulses in a Mahdfel's life were to battle and to breed. His mate brought him joy. He was not ashamed to indulge her.

Was his indulgence detrimental to the clan? Did he play it too safe, too conservative? While his need to breed was more than satisfied, and the number of mates in the clan grew daily, the need for battle was ignored. In the last year they had one raid and destroyed two Suhlik research facilities.

Paax stroked his chin. It was not enough. A good, hard fight would take the edge off. He'd speak with Mylomon but first his mate required him.

"Sir?" The medic voice, thin over the device, roused Paax from his thoughts. Often his mind saw patterns and made connections. Each connection was a new possibility and he chased down that possibility to its conclusion, but such introspection made him quiet and he forgot to share his conclusions. Some warriors trusted that he arrived at the correct conclusion. Others stared at him, baffled.

"On my way."

In the corridor, the unmistakable rasp of a blade being unsheathed rang out.

Paax paused but did not turn to face his challenger. To sneak up from behind was cowardly and he would not acknowledge such a low attempt.

He wore no armor and carried no weapon himself. The head of security, Seeran, hounded him to remedy that but

Paax believed that if dressed as if he expected to battle his crew, they wouldn't disappoint him.

There was no good solution. Dress for battle, expect a challenge. Dress to avoid battle, appear weak and vulnerable, and expect a challenge. This was the never ending problem his brother left behind for him.

"Be certain before you act," Paax said, voice carrying. He might be unarmed, but he was far from helpless.

The sword was sheathed and the would-be attacker retreated.

Paax still did not turn. He did not need to see Antu's backside to know it was the hot-headed male who nearly attacked.

He had to do something about the growing dissent in the clan, sooner rather than later. But first, his mate needed him.

HIS LITTLE STAR sat on an exam table, tissues in hand and her pale Terran face streaked from crying. Wrapped in the oversized Sangrin-styled robe, she had an uncanny resemblance to his mother.

Kalen's female spoke to his mate, voices low. Whatever the female said, a smile briefly flashed across his little star's face.

All at once Paax was a child again, helpless to ease the suffering of a loved one, and his mother suffered. She seemed to be forever great with child, always pregnant. Despite her smiles and the hugs for her sons, her weary body ached. Every pregnancy was more difficult than the last. Every child she grew wore on her body, stealing away her vitality and, eventually, her life.

He should go to her and comfort her but his feet remained rooted in place.

Paax pulled Kalen to the side. "How is she?"

"Emotional," Kalen said in a huff. "But that is not unusual for a Terran female."

"And the—"

"Stable. Strong heartbeats. No unusual readings."

"No signs of incompatibility?"

"We would have seen that earlier. At this stage, we need to monitor her organ functions and blood pressure. Her body has undergone a great amount of stress and Terrans are fragile."

He glanced over the medic's shoulder at his mate, so small and yet so mighty. Had his father worried so over his mate and her endless pregnancies?

"You made it," Mercy said, a smile lighting up her face. It took so little to make his mate happy, just time. He desperately wanted to have more time to give her.

"The medic says you are healthy."

"The medic says a lot of things," Mercy said, rubbing her

belly absently, "but what he doesn't say is more important. I'm overdue and no one will admit it."

"Your pregnancy is progressing normally," Kalen said, back stiff but voice even stiffer.

"This kid should have been out of me days ago."

"The gestation is within an acceptable timeframe."

They would bicker at each other endlessly if Paax did not put a stop to it now. He put a hand on the small of her back, rubbing a calming circle. Tense muscle relaxed under his touch. "Is my mate free to go?"

"Yes. I will reevaluate tomorrow."

"So that's it?" Mercy narrowed her eyes. "Yesterday you had to take blood."

"That was yesterday," Kalen said.

Paax helped Mercy off the table, all the while she grumbled about doctors with the bedside manner of a bedpan. He took her back to their quarters and put her to bed with kisses and the promise that he would be there when she woke.

"You work too much," she said, adjusting the pillows surrounding her on the bed.

He worked to keep her safe, to keep their sons safe.

Son.

He frowned. He needed to control his thoughts better, lest he give her cause to worry.

"There is something I need to do before our son arrives," he said, repositioning the pillows at her back. She sighed and snuggled in.

"No one will tell me when I'm due and it's driving me crazy."

"These things are—"

"Hard to predict. Yeah, I've heard that before. Wake me when you come back. I want a good night kiss."

Paax leaned in, the scent of her clouding his senses in the best way. "I can kiss you now."

"You should," she agreed, lifting her face.

His lips brushed hers softly. He held himself back, gentle and patient.

Mercy grabbed him by the collar and pulled him forcefully down to her. "Don't go soft on me now, warrior."

Never.

The kiss deepened and grew urgent. It grew harder to leave her, even for moment, with her hands tugging on the shirt like it offended her.

Mercy pulled away, lips swollen and a deep pink. "That was a see-you-later kiss. Wake me up for your proper good night kiss."

He wouldn't miss that for all the stars in the sky.

The *Judgment* ran on a twenty-four-hour schedule with constant shift rotation, but the lights dimmed to simulate a night cycle. Paax stalked through the darkened corridors, passing crew who did not look him in the eye. Was that the proper amount of respect or total lack of respect.

Perhaps the warriors were not the only one in need of a solid fight.

The double guessing needed to end. Paax made himself a mug of steaming tea before summoning Mylomon to his ready room. The male's sharp eyes noticed the crystal beads on the table. Paax had been trying to construct a pendant but the wires were fidgety and his fingers not as nimble as they used to be. Progress was slow as he would only rest when the pendant was flawless.

"Tea?" Paax asked. The pungent green scent reminded him of home.

Mylomon looked at the mug in Paax's hand with suspicion. "No."

Paax took a sip. Sharp and bitter, the tea could not be described as pleasant. "It's an acquired taste."

Mylomon shifted, betraying his unease. "Is there a reason you called me so late into my rest cycle?"

"Yes. Sit. Tomorrow we will do two things. One, we will move the *Judgment* deeper into Suhlik territory."

"The council has not—"

"The council merely advises a warlord, they do not dictate." The council would advise the *Judgment* to remain in neutral space, but was it violating orders if communications were down? Ask no questions, tell no lies. He always liked that Terran phrase.

"You've already decided on coordinates."

Paax transmitted the location to Mylomon. The male glanced at his wrist comm to confirm what he already knew. Several months ago the clan raided a Suhlik research facility. The data specialists were able to recover communications which hinted at other hidden research facilities. Paax wanted to hunt down the possible sites and eradicate the Suhlik's vile "science" but the council encouraged him to remain in place. The council didn't forbid him, as if they could forbid a warlord from anything, but they did not sanction it, either.

"This location will require several weeks of travel." Meaning the council would notice if the *Judgment's* excursion.

"There is a Gate near Alva. It will reduce our travel time." Gates, teleportation devices large enough for spacecraft, linked Mahdfel territory and planets. Massive interstellar distances became nothing more than brief journey and what one took months now took days, possibly hours. They required a security code to activate. The Alva Gate was far enough away that he could reach it before the council realized the *Judgment* was gone and deactivate his security code. The timing would be close but it was doable.

"And our warriors on Earth?"

The pilot was useful but not vital. Seeran, his chief of security, was vital. "We'll finish our missions before they leave Earth."

The dark male nodded. "A fight will be beneficial for the clan. They grow restless."

"The second point, I will call a gathering for our warriors in the arena." Paax paused, waiting for his second-in-command's reaction.

"You expect a challenge."

"I invite a challenge." Better now, on his terms, than later when he was not prepared or distracted. His mate would give birth any day now. If he were an ambitious male, that's when he would strike, when the warlord was occupied with his mate.

"Mercy will not like it," Mylomon said at length.

Paax nodded. Mercy did not like many things but this was their reality. Yes, his life would be simpler if he was still a scientist in his lab but there was nothing to be gained from wasting energy on the wishful thinking. He was the warlord. He needed to cement his leadership in place to secure the safety of his mate and their soon-to-be-born children.

"What do we tell her?"

"Mercy does not need to know."

Mylomon frowned. "Terran females like to be informed of decisions, even ones that they cannot influence or change."

"That knowledge will only worry her and her health is delicate enough." Mercy would only worry if she knew.

Better to say nothing than be cornered into a lie or admitting the truth.

Paax swirled the remaining tea in the cup, sediment from the tea leaves settled at the bottom of the amber liquid. His gut protested that it was wrong to keep this from his mate but his reason told him it was for the best.

Yes, this was best.

CHAPTER 3

Paax

His mate slept.

In the dim light, the luminescence of her womb cast a soft glow on her features. She was so beautiful. After a year, he could not believe his luck in being matched to such a lovely mate. He'd never grow tired of admiring her and she grew lovelier each day.

Paax admired the way her dark hair spilled across the white bed linens. Her body curled around a large pillow. He wanted to climb in the bed, run his hand up her shapely calves and soft thighs and cup the round swell of her ass, wake her and demonstrate his devotion, but he knew sleep was a precious rarity for her. He would not disturb her slumber.

He kept the knowledge that she carried twins secret from her and he knew she would be upset if she found out. When she found out. The probability of losing a baby was high. He had seen his mother go through that suffering enough times to want to spare his mate. Yes, she had been healthy until this point and yes, all the scans came back within acceptable limits, but delivery was the most dangerous time and Terrans were so small.

If the worst happened and they lost a child, then she would be spared the painful knowledge. She could not mourn what she did not know she lost. A painful decision to be sure but for the best.

As if sensing his presence, Mercy stirred awake. She rolled onto her back and smiled up at him.

"What's that look for?" she asked, voice thick with sleep.

Paax leaned in and planted a soft kiss on her forehead. "Just imaging what our sons will look like."

"Sons, huh?"

Paax paused, waiting for her reaction.

"You assume I'm willing to do this again." She patted her belly, eyes sparking with mischief. "I mean, I love you but this is work. I'm going to need some convincing."

"Convincing, huh," he repeated, tone mocking the lilt in her voice. He crawled into the bed on all fours, prowling toward her. "I think I can be very convincing."

Mercy giggled, and rolled to the side, using the blanket as protective cover. Paax pressed himself against her back, savoring the feel of her soft curves against him. He lifted her dark hair, exposing the slender column of her delectable neck. He pressed a kiss to the flesh, breathing deeply. She smelled so *good*. Better than good. Perfect, like the sweetest fruit on a summer's day, heavy with juice. He licked the back of her neck, the taste of her bursting on his tongue. He needed more. He ground his hardened cock into the curve of her ass. He needed her.

"You can't possibly want me now," Mercy said. "I'm huge."

"Mmm," Paax murmured, hands roaming over her sensitive breasts and belly. "You are succulent and ripe, ready to be plucked."

"Is that what you're going to do? Pluck me?"

"Do you need to be convinced?" He gently squeezed a nipple and she arched against him, moaning.

She angled her head, lifting her mouth to his. Her lips, pink and succulent, begged to be captured. He claimed her mouth in a bruising kiss, full of intensity and need. Her hand drifted up and stroked down the length of his horn, finger curling around the base. He growled and his tattoos burned.

He tore his lips away and pressed his mouth against the base of her neck. Her enticing scent was strongest here. Breathing deep, he just couldn't get enough. He licked and nipped, hands cupped the delicious weight of her breasts and she responded enthusiastically.

He brushed her stomach, the tender swell of her belly and ran a finger under her panties.

One leg wedged between her thighs, lifting them just enough for his free hand to slide down her soaked panties.

"You shouldn't wear these," he growled. His fingers slipped into her curls, pleased to find her ready and as needy as him. Pregnancy hormones increased her desire but he was cautioned that the effect would wear off. It never did.

His fingers slid over her sensitive button, eliciting another moan as she ground her ass into him. So responsive. He stroked the length of her pink slit before pushing two fingers into her. Hot and tight, she clamped down on him, rocking her hips. She rode his hand to completion, shuddering and sighing.

Paax licked his fingers clean. "Ripe and juicy."

A small chuckled escaped from the back of her throat.

His fingers hooked over the elastic of her panties and he pulled them down. She shimmied out of her clothing as he did the same. Finally nude, he pressed himself against her soft back. His mate was lush, soft and warm. He lifted one thigh over his own and cupped her pussy, still hot and wet and ready for him.

His cock lined up at her pink and swollen entrance. He paused.

"I need you," she said, which was all the encouragement he needed.

Paax surged into his mate, filling her deeply. Hot and wet and so tight, he pumped into her, pushing until he bottomed out and she gave a little squeak. He pulled back, savoring every inch as his cock moved out and then back again. In this moment he didn't need words and the worries of leading a clan fell away. There was only him and his little star, his mate, his wife and perfection. Her body fit his. She moved with him without direction, instinctively matching his pace. Her coos and moans inflamed his desire, driving his pleasure to greater heights.

She tilted her head back, hands reaching for his horn, and she smiled.

Her smile eased the ache in his heart and he didn't want the moment to end.

Her climax broke. She rippled around him, squeezing and milking him. He couldn't last much longer. He pumped into her two, three more times before emptying.

Mercy rolled to face him. His tattoos glowed in the dim light and her fingers traced the pattern, reading them. "I'm going to miss this."

"Eh?" He nuzzled the curve of her neck, where the scar from his claiming bite gleamed against her skin. She had a perfect neck, slender enough for his hand to wrap around the back and sensitive. He lapped at the scar and she sighed.

"This. You crawling into bed and having your wicked way with me." A finger danced along the curve of his horn, hardly touching him at all. Her hand went toward the stump of his amputated horn. The nub regrew slowly and the material there, normally sensitive, was especially so. As an adolescent, his horns grew with changing hormones and were tender to every sensation and those sensations went directly to his cock. A stiff breeze could make him hard. Had, in fact. Once his horns grew in, Paax never expected to experience that particularly awkward torture again, but here he was in bed with his beautiful wife, her touch on his tender horn driving him mad.

"I told you, you're ripe and succulent. You inspire my hunger." His lips drifted down to the valley between her breasts. Their size had increased in the last few months and proved endlessly fascinating to him.

Mercy pushed his face away. "They're too sensitive."

Endlessly fascinating because he wasn't allowed to touch them. Much had changed on her body in the last year and he need to catalogue every red stretch mark, every new curve and new sensitivity. "When our son comes—"

"I'll need time to heal."

Paax stroked the swollen pink nipples. That wasn't what he was trying to ask but it was a good topic to pursue. "How long will you need to heal?"

"I don't know. I've never pushed a baby out my hoo-ha before. Six weeks, the doctor says."

Displeasure rumbled in his throat. He did not want his mate talking about sex with another male, even if it was the medic and even if it was to find out how soon they could partake after the birth of their sons.

She laughed. "That jealous streak of yours really shouldn't be hot but dang if I can't resist."

Mercy

. . .

PAAX STROKED HER HAIR, brushing back from her forehead and skimming the length of her dark brown locks all the way past her shoulders and down to the small of her back. His hand rested there, perfectly filling the slight curve. Here, in bed with his arms around her, she didn't feel any discomfort; just the warmth of his body next to hers.

"Have you given any more thought to the naming ceremony?" he asked.

While birthdays were a foreign concept to the Mahdfel, they did celebrate the birth of a son. Paax explained that the infant would be presented to the clan, given a warrior's name and marked with the sigil of their father. Normally it was a small, private affair for the family and close friends. Expectations for the warlord, however, were different, as they often were.

Baby's first tattoo, Mercy thought, not entirely sold on the idea. "Will it hurt him?"

"A warrior does not cry," Paax said.

"We're not talking about a warrior. We're talking about a baby."

He grunted a noncommittal response. Clearly he didn't see the difference.

"I don't want any part of some ceremony that's going to hurt our son," she said, pulling away from his embrace.

"The skin is numbed. There is no sensation."

"Really? Or are you just saying that to appease me?"

He pulled her back down, pressing her back to his chest. "Truth. I'm not interested in hurting our son, either."

"At least we agree on that."

"Have you thought of any names?"

Mercy closed her eyes and sighed. For the last month, they'd gone round and round on names and were no closer to naming their son than when they started. Paax gave her a list of his family names and she vetoed the obviously terrible ones. Pinnis? Really? Paax still didn't understand what was wrong with the name when she explained.

She wasn't being spiteful. He did the same with her list. Human names were "weak", apparently, and no warrior would respect a Michael with a straight face. She didn't know why. Michael was a fantastic name.

"I still don't know what's wrong with Michael," she said, rolling over to face her husband.

"Because *mikael* means sugar in my language. No warrior will fear Sugar."

"I think you're being small minded about this, honey. I think a warrior called Sugar is terrifying."

His bright blue eyes narrowed, as if trying to ascertain if she were joking or not.

Mercy smiled and patted his shoulder. "Joking, honey-buns." He was solid muscle under her hand, unmoving as stone. His body had changed much in their year of marriage, as did hers. She grew softer, rounder. He grew harder, gained muscle mass and definition. Paax had been a scientist when they were married, before he became warlord. He wasn't a slouch then, with a lean, athletic build. All Mahdfel were warriors, even the scientists. His training, however, had not been as intense.

Becoming warlord changed that. Mercy knew Paax trained daily, sometimes twice. He needed to be in top form because a warlord led with his physical prowess as well as through his strategic superiority.

Her hand drifted down his shoulder, gliding over his pec and toward the solid washboard abs. One year or twenty, she'd never get tired of this view.

Paax raised an eyebrow. "Were you not satisfied, little star? Do I need to improve my performance?"

"Hmm? Oh," she blushed. "Sorry. I got distracted."

"Not what a male wants to hear from his mate." Paax rolled her until she sat astride him. "Obviously I need to practice my form."

Mercy licked her lips as his muscles bunched and flexed under her. No, there was nothing wrong with his form. "I really do want to talk about baby names."

"We talk and talk but come to no consensus." He lifted his hip ever so slightly and she felt the poke of his already hard cock.

"Are you even serious right now?"

Another thrust. "Very. My mate needs to be plucked.

Again."

"Help me name this kid and we can pluck our brains out."

Paax growled and Mercy tingled at the sound.

"Seriously, don't do that," she said.

"Do what? This?" A growl and a thrust and a shot of pure desire ran through her body.

"That. This kid will be here any day now and all we have is a long, long list of vetoed names."

"We will know his name when we see him."

Right. She was so not interested in that scenario. "I'll name him Rover if you don't give me a better alternative."

"Rover is interesting—"

"No! It's a dog's name."

"The rotic sound is aggressive and it implies travel. I like it."

Was he even being serious? His eyes gleamed and the barest hint of fang showed on his face. That jerk was trying to hide his laughter.

A smile spread over her face in response. It was good to see Paax laugh. He was so serious all the time. The pressures and expectations of being warlord meant Paax's public persona was gruff and serious. The clan demanded a stern warlord and frankly Mercy enjoyed a dominant hand, but it was good to see him relaxed and laughing, even if it was at her expense. "I'm sorry I mentioned it. Sheesh," she said with a dramatic eye roll.

"Nic," he offered.

"Nic Nawks? That's a hard no."

"Maax."

"That's a power level, not a name."

"Opportunity."

"Seriously? Did you not understand why Nic was vetoed?"

"Axil."

Mercy paused, considering it. "Yeah, that sounds all right. Axil."

"And Drake."

"Axil Drake Nawk? I didn't think you guys did middle names."

"Drake is a strong name. It is also your name." His hand roamed up her thighs and settled over the swell of her stomach. "So it is perfect."

That was so sweet and corny. She went all fluttery on the inside. "How long have you been holding onto that? Because I've been agonizing on a name for months."

"A few days." His thumbs rubbed small circles on her skin. A few days ago this position would have been too uncomfortable but the baby had shifted, sitting lower. This was nice.

"Wait— You've been feeding me terrible names on purpose."

He grinned, this time not bothering to hide his laughter.

CHAPTER 4

Paax

Paax left his mate sleeping, curled on her side. He dressed silently into his exo-armor. As he left the room, he pulled the blanket over her slumbering form and fought back the guilty mutter that he was sneaking away. If she knew what the day held in store, she'd beg him not to leave. He would, because there was no choice. His warriors needed to see their warlord challenged and defeat those challengers. There was no avoiding it.

Mylomon waited in the shadows of the common room.

Paax nodded at the male and said nothing. Doors, locked or otherwise, were hardly a hindrance to him.

Weapons were mounted on a wall. Before Paax was warlord, the display was largely aesthetic. While proficient in all the weapons, he was a scientist and rarely used them outside of training.

Much had changed in the last year.

His fingers skimmed along the handle of a war axe. He found the weapon's utility appealing.

"That one? Really?"

Paax said nothing but added the axe to the harness on his back. Next he selected the short sword with the blue energized edge. This weapon had long been his favorite. The blade never lost its wickedly sharp edge. The length and the weight felt natural in his hands, like an extension of himself.

It was the blade that made him warlord.

It was the blade that killed his brother.

He added the blade to his harness. He could not afford to become sentimental today, not if he wanted to return to his mate and greet his sons.

Mylomon checked the straps on the harness and the seams on the armor, even though the nanite carbon fiber was seamless. "No helmet?"

"I've lost one horn. Losing the other will only improve my balance." Horns were such a symbol of virility, or strength, that to have one amputated in battle was akin to losing your manhood. Most males shuddered at the sight but Paax was not ashamed. It was the price he paid to become warlord and his horn would regrow. Eventually.

The male grinned, a slash of white fang against his dark complexion. If anyone understood what it was like to flaunt a shameful weakness and turn it into an asset, it was Mylomon. For the longest time, the male had no tattoos: no family, no clan, no place in the universe and it unnerved the other warriors.

"Antu's brother will demand revenge," Mylomon said.

"This is our way." There was no question that Antomas would have to accept his brother's defeat. The male drew a blade on his warlord. He would not be able to resist an open challenge today. Yes, Paax baited Antu but the fight would be fair. No tricks. Brawn and brains would win out in the end. It was the Mahdfel way. Antomas did not have to like it but he had to accept it.

If a warlord could not accept the defeat of another, even a brother, in combat, then that would put his own leadership in jeopardy. Antomas had little choice, much as Paax did. He had to call out Antu, invite the male to battle him, or the whispers of dissent would grow to all out mutiny. And then who would protect his Mercy? His sons? No one. The Suhlik would slaughter his mate, seize his sons and enslave them.

Antu left him no choice at all.

Mercy

IN THE MORNING, Mercy prepared for an autopsy. The party she organized last month for the newly arrived wives and their mates did not go as planned. Disaster was a good way to describe it. She needed to slice open that disaster and examine what went wrong.

Mercy intended the party to be social mixer for the new wives to get to know each other. The Mahdfel interpreted "party" to mean a competition. Newly matched males competed with each other to prove their worthiness as mates. The wrestling was fine. That was an actual sport and took skill. However, when the horned aliens started ramming each other, clashing horns, that's when Mercy shut the whole thing down. No music, some food, lots of wine, no chairs and alien warriors all too willing to strip down to their skivvies and show off their assets.

The party went sideways very quickly and Mercy had no idea why.

Dorothy helped Mercy out of bed and to dress. Lately she wore robes in the Sangrin style with wide sleeves. Comfort became her top priority with her expanding waistline and nothing was more comfortable than a silk robe with an adjustable belt.

She and her entourage headed to the dining hall. She could have meals delivered to her apartment but wanted the exercise. Paax forbade her from any strenuous activity and all the rest of the Mahdfel acted as if she were made of spun glass. Walking remained a permissible activity and she wasn't about to give it up, even though her ankles swelled and her back ached.

Entering the dining hall, every horned head turned in her direction. A strange awareness crawled over her. The warriors of the clan did not see *her*, they just saw her belly. She wasn't even a person to them, just a symbol of their warlord's prowess.

The ship's cook, Dannel, an older male with iron grey hair and horns nearly black with age, waved her over to a table. Her breakfast companion waited and the table was over burdened with dishes.

"Warlord's female," Dannel said, with a slight bow of his head. He then turned to her mother. "Dorothy Drake." He did not bow. His eyes held Dorothy's until the older woman blushed. She tucked her hair behind an ear and looked away quickly.

Mercy raised an eyebrow, fighting the urge to ask her mother what that was all about. Her father, Dorothy's husband, died during the invasion many years ago. She didn't really expect her mother to spend the rest of her days alone but she didn't really expect to see her mother flirting with an alien, either.

Daisy sat at the table, blonde curls loose about her shoulders but dressed in her nurse scrubs, completely riveted by the flirting. Her hands propped up her chin. "Oh my God, that is adorable."

"That's my mother," Mercy said, lowering herself to the table. Braith scrambled to help her with the chair but she waved him away.

"And it's adorable. Are you two dating, Dorothy?" she asked, turning her attention away from the mortified Mercy to the blushing Dorothy. "I know you're too old for the match, but can a Mahdfel age out the way a human can? What are you going to do if you love him and he gets matched to someone else? Oh my God, that's going make me cry."

Dorothy snapped up the cloth napkin and spread it on her lap with precision. "I don't know. He'd have to speak more than two words to me, so let's not get too excited."

Daisy giggled with delight but Mercy just wanted to sink through the floor. She wanted to talk about anything other than her mother's love life. "Heading to medical after this?"

Please change the topic. Please.

Daisy nodded. "My shift starts in an hour. You're looking well."

"You don't have to lie. I look tired and bloated."

"I thought pregnant women were supposed to glow?"

"Oh, I glow at night." Mercy rubbed her belly unconsciously. "This little fella lights up the room."

Daisy wrinkled her nose. "That can't be good for you."

"Meridan says it's normal."

"She would know." Daisy poured them each a cup of coffee. She added cream and sugar before handing the cup to Mercy.

The breakfast meal was a heaping plate of fried dough balls stuffed with either fruit or savory ground meat. Deep in a craving, Mercy tried to explain the concept of a pierogi to Dannel and the ball of fried dough is what he served. The fruit was his own spin, in addition to the dipping sauces.

"It's not quite a pierogi," Dorothy said, spearing one ball

on the end of a fork. "I should teach Dannel how to make them."

Daisy and Mercy shared a glance. "Can you make tamales? Because my mother use to make the best tamales but I never got the knack."

"I could try," Dorothy said. "The cook is skilled but he needs some instruction on Earth cuisine."

Daisy nudged Mercy's foot under the table and wiggled her eyebrows.

Mercy rolled her eyes, ignoring the woman, and placed three of the flour dusted balls on her plate. She had no idea what she selected until she cut into them but the mystery was part of the appeal. It was exotic and comforting at the same time.

Daisy bit into hers and wrinkled her nose. "Yeast spread," she said, dropping the ball.

The pungent and meaty aroma hit her and Mercy's stomach growled. She grabbed the yeast filled ball, savoring the salty taste. It was almost like marmite, which Mercy would have never touched on Earth. Pregnancy cravings were so weird.

Daisy said nothing. Her husband was Mylomon, the second in command of the clan. As a result, they spent much time in each other's company. That wasn't the first yeast ball Mercy had grabbed right off her plate.

As much as Mercy didn't care for Mylomon, she rather liked his wife. She was sunny and chatty where Mylomon was grim and silent. Mercy knew her opinion of Mylomon was too harsh but they had started out on the wrong foot, too. He had stabbed her, for crying out loud. Less than two days married to Paax and the previous warlord had ordered Mylomon to wound her. He followed orders. That's what a warrior did.

Unfortunately, those orders happened to suck. Still, he did help Paax defeat Omas in battle. She should reevaluate her opinion of him. In the last year, Mylomon had worked tirelessly for Paax and Daisy seemed happy in their marriage. Perhaps he wasn't all bad, stabbing aside.

"What's that look for?" Daisy asked.

"I was just wondering why the dining hall is empty," Mercy replied quickly. The dining hall was suspiciously void of warriors. Normally the large room was filled around the clock with warriors. The *Judgment* ran on a twenty-four hour schedule with no day or night cycles. Someone was always coming on or off shift. "Braith? Kleve?" She turned to her security detail but the males shook their head.

"I am unsure, warlord's female," Kleve said. "The warlord called many to the arena."

"So you boys are having a secret meeting? Why aren't you three there?"

Braith, Kleve and Jolyon looked at each other, confusion on their faces. "We must remain with you," Kleve finally said.

Fair enough.

Mercy turned her attention back to Daisy and the cup of

decaf coffee. The flavor and the ritual of preparing a cup satisfied her craving but dang if she didn't miss caffeine. Soon. "Tell me why my party sucked."

"Suck is a harsh word," Daisy said diplomatically.

"It sucked. I thought there were lots of parties at the moon base so why didn't my party work?"

She shrugged. "The social events were a human/Mahdfel hybrid. I think the rec department mashed up Earth and Mahdfel holidays."

"But it was a party, right? With music and dancing and no… horn butting."

"Yes, but the rec department is mostly human. The population of the moon base is half human, half Mahdfel. Here, we're—"

"Outnumbered."

"I was going to say under represented. You planning another party?"

Mercy sipped the coffee, savoring the sweet and acrid taste. "When you arrived on the *Judgment,* what was your experience like?"

"Hectic." Daisy shook her head. "It's all a blur, really."

"I want to do something for the new wives. An orientation. Right now we're relying on the males to get them to medical and get their security clearances but there's no good protocol."

"Does everything need a protocol?"

Mercy remembered the anxiety and confusion she felt after teleporting across the universe to her new husband. "Yes. They should know they're not alone here."

"Hmm. If you have the new brides go straight into an orientation process with another male, I think the newly mated men would lose their minds."

The need to protect a mate was hardwired into the Mahd-fel. Separation from a mate had serious consequences, especially early in the relationship. At least that's what every pacing, snarling male said once they learned of their match and impatiently waited for her arrival. Just knowing a match existed flipped a switch in their brain, turning them from easy-going into over-protective beast.

"So have a woman do the orientation," Dorothy said. "It doesn't have to be immediate. Couldn't you do it two or three days after arrival."

Sensible and reasonable. The female population grew daily. While she'd like to personally greet every new bride, she just wasn't physically able. She'd search for a volunteer, someone with a warm smile and comforting manner. Mercy opened her mouth to say as much when a cramp rolled through her stomach, followed by a popping sensation and a release of pressure. Water gushed out from between her legs.

She sat stunned, briefly mortified that she lost control of her bladder and peed everywhere. Then she realized that the volume was too much. Her water had broken.

Finally.

Mercy's grabbed her mother's wrist and scanned the room to see if her guards were nearby. They were close but not within earshot if she spoke softly.

"What is it?" Dorothy asked.

"I need everyone to stay calm," she said in a quiet voice, nearly a whisper.

"When you say things like that, it makes me not calm."

"Don't shout and don't get excited, but I need to go to medical."

Daisy immediately tapped out a message on her comm unit. "OK, Meridan knows we are on our way. Are you having contractions?"

Mercy rubbed her belly, waiting. "I don't know."

Dorothy helped her up from the chair. "We're not going to panic. We're going to walk calmly to medical."

Braith apparently heard every word. Dang that superior alien hearing. "Warlord's female, you are in medical distress."

"I'm not in distress. I'm in labor."

"We will go to medical. Now." Braith moved to lift her into his arms.

She batted his hands away. "I can still walk."

"The distance is far and you are compromised."

"I'm not compromised."

"Is that the normal volume of fluid?" Jolyon asked, staring at the growing puddle on the floor. "That's rather a lot."

"How do we cease the purge of fluid?" Kleve turned to Daisy, the only qualified medical practitioner in the room. "Tell us, female."

"I'm going to medical and no one is carrying me," Mercy said, voice growing firm.

"Unacceptable." Braith and Kleve exchanged a look and moved at the same time, pinning her between their muscular frames. She was trapped. So not fair.

"You're making me upset," she warned, trying to duck their arms. "And Paax won't be happy when I tell him." Yes, it was a dirty trick, threatening to tattle on her guys but it was the only trick she had.

"The warlord will be more upset if we allowed you to injure yourself."

"Good point. Why don't you go ask him how he feels?" Mercy pointed over Kleve's shoulder. When the male turned, she ducked away, surprisingly nimble for a woman in labor.

She made it exactly two steps before Braith scooped her up. She huffed in frustration. "Fine. If you have to carry me, make it snappy."

CHAPTER 5

Paax

Mediation grounded him. Before a great trial of his intellect or physical skill, Paax always took the time to find his center and breathe. In his youth, other warriors had scoffed at his methods. They preferred to work themselves into a frenzy.

Frenzies were not precise. Paax was unfailingly precise. He had never failed a trial. When he decided to master something, he did. When challenged, he was triumphant. There was no alternative.

Today would be no different.

Every day started in the training arena, as it had since he'd begun his warrior's training as a child. While he remained a scientist first, the other males forgot that he was also a warrior. He let them remain ill-informed. Their lazy observations only served to help him, and he enjoyed the look of shock in their eyes when they realized they had vastly underestimated him.

Paax heard the rumors, the whispers saying he was unfit to be warlord, that Omas had been weak and only a lucky blow took the former warlord's life. Any warrior could have done it. Any warrior could take the new warlord.

Paax was neither deaf or blind.

Today the rumors and whispers stopped.

He'd separate the gossiping males from his clan, the ones who only recognized brute strength as the most important virtue in a leader. He'd leave behind only those who valued intellect *and* physical prowess. He'd take on the entire clan if required to ensure the safety and wellbeing of his mate and children. There was no alternative.

He'd start with that arrogant communications officer, Antu, who thought he deserved preferential treatment because his brother happened to be the warlord of another clan. Antu only valued brute strength. His brother, Antomas, was disappointingly the same. Raw physical strength might win the warlord's command, but it could not hold onto it. Antomas would find out soon enough.

Antu fancied himself worthy to lead the *Judgment*. Paax heard those rumors, too. Empty words, spouted by an empty-headed male. Soon he'd make it clear that there were consequences for empty words.

Paax caught his reflection in the glossy surface of the wall paneling. Omas stared back at him.

The changes had happened so slowly over the course of

the last year that Paax had failed to notice. Their similarities lied more than just in their identical jaw and hair; it reflected in the hard glint in his eye.

He was unsure how this made him feel. Connected to his twin as they shared the same burden of leading the clan? Resentful that Omas pushed this burden on him? Thankful that Omas brought a mate to Paax at long last?

If he were still alive, they'd spar and purge the bad feelings out, stopping only when their muscles ached and the vitriol between them vanished. Antu would have to do.

Paax surveyed the arena. A good number of males arrived, curious. Other's had the lean, anticipatory look of predators about them. They smelled blood in the water.

The crowd fell silent.

Paax strode into the center. He wasn't one for a spectacle, preferring to get down to it. He took off his armor piece by piece, letting them fall to the sand floor. He wore only loose fitting trousers, no shirt and no shoes. The sand of the arena floor worked its way between his toes.

"I won't waste our time with a speech. You know why you are here. Those who believe they can best their warlord should do so now."

A male, lean and young, climbed over the retaining wall. He dropped to a crouch, eyes gleaming at Paax with ambition.

Fool.

Paax rushed in, slicing a tendon before he had a chance to

stand. The youth rolled onto his back. To his credit he did not cry out. He swallowed his pain and that saved his life.

The point of his sword pressed into the prone male's throat. "Do you concede?"

"Yes, warlord."

Paax eased back the sword, allowing the male to regain his footing and hobble away. The wound was not critical. He would heal.

Another male approached, this one less dramatic and cock-sure in his approach. Paax recognized him as staff for navigation. A supporter of Antu, then, and possible saboteur.

"You are weak, Paax Nawk," the male said. "You sit and think and do nothing, like a weakling."

He mistook intelligence and planning for weakness. The *Judgment* was better off without a male like him.

The male rushed forward, sword swinging wide overhead. Dumb and sloppy. Paax blocked with one hand and side stepped. As the male spun, Paax's war hammer knocked his legs out from underneath him.

"Do you concede?"

"Never." The male spat.

Paax moved with brutal efficiency and ran his sword through the warrior's throat, pinning him to the sandy arena floor. Barely a moment passed before he felt the air move as Antu approached in a shameless, honorless move. He spun, blocking the blow aimed for his back.

Antu moved swiftly, youth and righteous vigor on his side. They danced across the sand, exchanging blows. The energy imbued edges of their weapons humming and crackling with each clash.

"You are old," Antu said, forcing Paax back.

The edge of the blade grazed his temple, drawing blood. The pain stung but he ignored it for the moment. He let the male gain the upper hand because the truth was that Paax was older. Racing around the arena wore him down. Antu had youth on his side and could run and jump and make all sorts of attention grabbing displays. It was all show and no substance.

Antu was cocky and sloppy, his stance unbalanced and leaning too far forward.

"Nothing to say?" With a grin he drove forward in a series of blows, each swing becoming grander and flashier. Paax kept his motions simple, expending just enough energy to block, moving just enough to avoid the blade, and retaining his balance. Even the fast flurry of Antu's blows did not unsettle his footing. He moved when he chose to move.

His sword had a shortened reach, allowing Antu in closer. The male lunged forward aggressively, blade piercing Paax's shoulder. Armor would have stopped that.

Paax wrapped his hand around the blade, the edge cutting into his palm. He yanked the blade out of his shoulder. Shocked, Antu's grip on the hilt loosen. "How can you?"

Paax yanked the blade away entirely. Antu stared down at his empty hands, shocked that his weapon vanished.

"Do you know why I took off my armor?" Paax asked.

Antu fell to his knees. Weaponless due to his own hubris, he was dead. If Paax had pity and spared his life, he was still the warrior who let go of his weapon. Another warrior would remove the blight of his shame at the first opportunity. A Mahdfel did not let go of his weapon, be it a sword or a rifle, in combat. Ever.

"I did it so vainglorious idiots like yourself would believe they had the upper hand and be lazy. Lazy loses battles. Lazy costs lives." He shouted the words to his wider audience of warriors. Paax pressed the blade to Antu's throat. "*Always* ask why the enemy does what he does." It was too late for Antu to learn battle tactics now.

"Mercy," Antu whispered.

"Yes," Paax agreed. "That is why we are here." She was the motivation for everything.

The energy imbued blade sliced through the male's neck, head spinning clean off and landing in the sand.

CHAPTER 6

Mercy

This was real life. Not a movie or a show, but real and really happening to her. She was in labor. She was about to be a mom.

Muscles deep in her pelvis cramped, twisted and the pain radiated out to her lower back, seizing the muscles up tight. As the contraction eased, the pain dissipated the way it arrived. The pain distracted her and kept her from panicking. From the moment Braith darted down the corridors of the *Judgment* and into medical, Kleve and Jolyon tried to reach Paax over the comm. He wasn't answering their calls.

Why wasn't he answering their calls?

Braith placed her on a bed just as a contraction hit. Mercy squeezed her eyes shut, preparing for the worst. The muscles in her pelvis cramped, not much worse than her regular menstrual cramp.

That was it? She looked over, caught her mother's concerned eyes, was about to say she didn't know what the big deal was, when her insides twisted.

The pain was blinding. Everything on the inside tried to punch itself way out of her. Mercy shouted and reached for Braith. He jerked back but she caught him by the horn, and squeezed. Squeezed so hard, until the tension inside her eased.

Braith staggered to his knees. "Warlord's female, please—"

While distracted, Kalen jabbed her with a needle. She barely noticed. "For pain," he said tersely.

Mercy released Braith. "Where is Paax?" Her voice was thin, already tired. This kid better come quick. She didn't know if she could endure hours of labor.

As if sensing her thoughts, Dorothy took her hand. "You're going to be fine, baby. You came flying out of me."

Mercy shuddered. Not helping. "Where is Paax?"

Braith, Kleve and Jolyon shared a look. "We're unable to reach him on comms," Jolyon said, slowly.

They were keeping something from her. Again. She was so sick of that behavior. What could be so bad that they couldn't tell her? Was Paax off fighting Suhlik somewhere? Was the ship under attack? Or were they trying to spare her precious little woman feelings because she was a delicate little flower and they didn't want her to worry.

She was sick of it. All of it.

Mercy waved Jolyon closer to the bed, plastering on her sweetest smile. The drugs were starting to work their way through her system so it wasn't hard to fake. His eyes went wide but he cautiously approached.

Her fist popped out and landed solidly at the base of his throat. Jolyon stumbled backward. Kleve and Dorothy held her by the shoulders, pinning her down. "You go find my husband and drag him back here! I don't know what you think you're not telling me, but you find Paax and find him now!"

Jolyon rubbed his throat and nodded, eyes wide with shock.

"Why are you just standing there? Go!" It took all her will not to leap out of the bed and thrash him. She wasn't a violent person, normally, but today she was willing to make an exception.

"If you're not related to the mother or my direct staff, get out of my surgery!" Kalen stormed in, all sound and fury.

"We have orders—"

Kalen cut off Braith. "I don't care. Get out. You can follow orders out of the room."

Braith huffed but didn't argue, instead turning to leave the crowded room. Kleve followed without complaint.

"Not as effective as your methods," he said, "but it'll suffice. How are you feeling?"

"I've been better," she said. "Whatever you gave me seems

to be working." She didn't hurt and felt almost disconnected from her body, as if floating on a tether.

The contraction came over her in a wave, the tether pulling taut and forcing her back down into her body. Gritting her teeth, Mercy clamped down on her mother's hand until the pain passed. Eventually only a dull, burning sensation remained in her lower back and pressure on her pelvis. And bladder.

"I need to pee," she said in a whisper to her mother.

"Don't worry about that now."

She didn't know when else she was supposed to worry about it.

The nurse appeared with a cup of water and pressed it to her lips. "Drink. You need the fluid. The pressure on your bladder is from the baby. It's not real."

"Feels real."

"Well, if you make a mess, I won't tell," she said with a wink.

"I don't care about a mess. I want my husband. Where is he?" Mercy turned to her mother, clutching her hand tightly.

"The men are looking for him now."

Meaning no one knew. The warlord was missing and his son's birth wasn't going to wait.

A machine beeped but it was almost pleasant, drifting into the background noise of the medical bay. There were so many machines. Meridan opened up the robe and the fabric fell away. She cleaned Mercy's exposed belly with a swab before sticking on a white pad.

"I'm cold," Mercy said.

"We'll get you covered in a minute," Meridan said. "We just need to hook you up to the monitor."

"Shouldn't you be looking at my cervix or something?"

"Oh, we're very interested in your cervix but we want to monitor your blood pressure, too." Meridan completed her task efficiently and covered Mercy in a light sheet, as promised.

More machines beeped. This time the noise was far from reassuring.

"Their heart rates are dropping," Kalen said. He placed a scanner directly on Mercy's stomach. He frowned.

"What's going on?" she asked. She tried to sit up to look at the screen but Kalen moved it away.

"The babies are in distress," he said. He turned to another medic, a male Mercy recognized but did not know the name of. "Prep for surgery."

"Babies? Surgery?"

Kalen patted her hand and gave her what he probably thought was a reassuring smile. It was all fangs and horrifying. "We need to get your sons out now. It seems they are too impatient to wait for your body to give birth the old-fashioned way."

Sons.

Plural.

Stunned, Mercy tried to formulate her questions. She looked to her mother, surprise also on her face.

Mercy didn't notice Kalen approaching with a mask until it was already over her mouth and nose. She swatted ineffectively at the air before slipping under into blackness.

Paax

PAAX GRIPPED the severed head by the hair and tossed it the nearest warrior. "Send this to his brother."

There would be repercussions. The Council would twist their hands and scold him but they were too frightened of the fury of a Mahdfel for Paax to consider them a serious threat. The council on Sangrin knew very well that it could not control the Mahdfel who pledged to protect the planet. At best, they directed the warlords' energies toward the Suhlik threat but they could not forbid two warlords determined to destroy one another. They could, however, take away the council seat they dangled in front of him for so long.

It did not matter. His decisions to pursue the Suhlik research facility ensured the council would not welcome him as an elder council member anytime soon.

Antomas was another issue. The minor warlord would

demand his revenge and there was nothing a council of soft Sangrin elders could do to stop it.

Paax needed to be prepared.

Jolyon approached him. The warrior was young and nervous but skilled and loyal, which is why Paax selected the male to guard his mate. "Warlord, sir—"

Paax swiped a cleansing cloth over his face, removing the dirt and gore. "Why are you not with my mate?"

"She sent me to fetch you—"

"Fetch me?"

The young warrior paled. Paax meant his words to be teasing but the male took them far too seriously. Jolyon's mouth opened and closed, no sound coming out. Mercy claimed the warrior was "funny" and "chatty." Paax saw no evidence to support her claim.

"Speak," Paax commanded.

"Your mate is in medical. She is laboring."

Labor.

His sons were being born.

He was a father.

"Is she well? And our sons?" Paax ran the cloth over his bare chest and arms, removing the worst of the blood. There was no time to don clothes.

"Yes, but she is calling for you. Demanding." Jolyon rubbed at his throat.

How could he ignore the demands of his wife?

He strode into medical, finding his worst nightmare. Braith and Kleve stood outside, removed by the head medic.

"Situation report," he snapped.

"Sir, we're unsure—"

Unsure? His mate's life and the lives of their twin sons required only certainty.

Paax dismissed them as useless and tried to enter the room. Mylomon's female barred him entry. "You have to wait out here," she said.

"I will see my mate. Now."

Daisy folded her arms over her chest. "No. They're in the middle of surgery. You can't just barge in there."

"You cannot stop me, female. Move. I do not wish to injure you."

"No!" Daisy stuck a hand out, landing her palm flat against stab wound on his shoulder.

He stared down at her hand and then at her, surprised that she would dare to touch him. "What is the meaning of this?"

"The babies heart rates dropped. They went into distress. It happens," she said. "Right now Kalen is performing an emergency c-section. She's in good hands."

Paax took a calming breath. "Explain this sea section."

"It's actually really common on Earth. Lots of women have the procedure and make full recoveries." She explained the procedure in detail.

"That's barbaric!" They cut open the womb and acted like it was normal. The medic had gutted his mate like a fish. "I must see her."

"Yeah, well you can't. You aren't exactly sterilized." She waved at his gore covered physique. "Is any of that your blood or is that a fashion statement?"

"Some."

"Let's sew you up, then."

More barbaric human medicine; sewing torn flesh with needle and thread like fabric. "No. I'll heal."

"I got news for you, Paax. If Mercy sees you looking like this, she's going to freak. Can you at least rinse off? You can use medical's cleansing room." Daisy pointed to the small room the medics used to sterilize themselves.

He glanced down at his hands, no longer his normal warm plum color but a dark, stained wine. If his mate saw him in such a state she would, indeed, freak. He did not want to greet the mother of his children with the blood of a lesser warrior on him. He would not hold his sons for the first time and blemish them in such a manner. "Agreed."

He quickly rinsed off and changed into a set of too-small scrubs. He sat quietly and suffered much insult to his dignity as Mylomon's female fused over his injuries. They would heal. Accelerated healing had been engineered into the Mahdfel genetic code. It would take much to seriously harm him and certainly much more than the wound Antu had inflicted.

He would heal. Mercy might not.

Kalen entered. He was not dressed in his normal crisp white lab coat but he wasn't covered in blood, either.

"Report," Paax said.

"You're mate is out of surgery, sir."

"And?" Paax ground his teeth, frustrated at both the female needlessly dressing his wounds and that no one would speak plainly and tell him what he burned to know. "Enough of this," he said, pulling his arm away from the nurse.

"You'll have a scar."

"Then I have a scar. Medic, speak now before I lose what precious control I have."

"Your mate is out of surgery."

"Has stress addled your brains?"

"And your sons are well."

"Both? Survived?" Twins. Such a rarity.

"They will be strong warriors."

Paax surged to his feet. "I must see them."

Kalen nodded. "I will allow you to view her only. Your mate is not to be disturbed."

The medics had placed a sleeping Mercy in an enclosed

room. The transparent walls tinged green allowed Paax to monitor her status. He paced, eyes always on her, flicking briefly to a screen and then back to her. Her dark hair was wet and plastered against her forehead. His little star seemed so small in the bed designed for a Mahdfel, swallowed up by the blankets and pillows.

How often had Paax stood in a very similar spot, helpless as he watched his mother recover from surgery? Too often. His mother was forever pregnant and they never went smoothly. Paax had been young but he remembered clearly his father pacing and snarling, threatening the medics, and demanding to hold his mate. Every child she carried left her a little bit more worn, a little bit more tired. So many brothers lost. After all those attempts, only Paax and Omas survived to adulthood.

Paax could still hear his mother's cries. Every child she lost broke her heart. Every single one.

And his heart hardened. Paax never wanted a mate. He never wanted to put a female through such pain and decided it was better to be alone. This was before the genetic compatibility test. His father, a good male and a strong warrior, selected his mother based on scent. She smelled good. Alluring.

Paax pressed his hand to the glass, willing himself closer. No matter how *good* or *alluring* his mother smelled, she was not a strong match to his father. They lost many children and, ultimately, her life.

His mother's struggle was exactly the reason Paax developed the genetic compatibility test. He wanted to spare all females the dangers of a risky pregnancy.

Mercy was a strong match, very compatible, and she held his heart, but she still required surgery. His best efforts to spare another female suffering, failed.

"She is strong," Kalen said.

"She suffered."

"Only because you were not here."

Paax narrowed his eyes at the medic. Sometimes he forgot how young and hot headed the male was. "You very well know where I was and what I had to do." For her. For their sons. Their safety was paramount.

Meridan and Daisy appeared, each carrying a swaddled bundle.

His heart pounded and blood thundered in his ears as Meridan placed his son in the cradle of his arms.

Words alone were not enough to express the joy surging through his body.

Impossibly small, his son fit in one hand. Paax's index finger ran over the infant's brow, feeling for a bump or ridge but finding only soft skin under dark, downy hair. His complexion was a vivid pink. Mercy would have the perfect name for it, flamingo or watermelon or some other Terran word, but Paax was satisfied with pink. The twins' complexions would darken in a few days. Even if they did not, they were perfect.

The infant grabbed Paax's finger, his tiny pink hand

clamping around his plum digit, and pulled it toward his mouth with surprising force.

There was nothing Paax would not do to ensure the safety of his son. No task was too onerous. No burden too great to bear. His little star had given him the greatest gift, *twice*.

"Ready for the other one, papa?" Daisy asked, placing the infant in the crook of Paax's empty arm. "What will you call them?"

Axil and Drake.

He knew their names in his heart but would wait for Mercy to wake. "It is the mother's honor to name a son."

"They look more Terran than I expected," Kalen said.

"Are Terrans this color at birth?"

Meridan cleared her throat. "Depends. Babies are normally a dark red or purple until they start to breath."

Paax looked at Kalen with alarm. "My sons are breathing, yes?"

"Relax," she continued. "I just meant that the skin tone normally changes. Totally normal for a human."

"But my sons are Mahdfel." His sons. His reality forever changed by two such small beings. The sensation of his heart expanding and strengthening all at once was so strange. "When will my mate awaken?"

"Her vitals are stable," Kalen said. "She should wake within an hour."

"Will she be in pain?"

Kalen shared a look with Meridan. "Not excessively."

"Unacceptable."

The son in the crook of his left arm cried out. Paax frowned. Was his voice too loud? Did he grip the infant too tightly? What was that foul odor? Had he hurt his son and already failed as a parent.

Meridan plucked the mewling baby away. "Time to change a diaper, I think."

"Show me how this thing is done. I will conquer it." The trials of fatherhood were strenuous but he would prevail.

CHAPTER 7

Mercy

Familiar and beloved vivid blue eyes waited for her when she woke. So many thoughts swirled through her, she didn't know where to start.

A huge bloody gash marred his forehead. Might as well start with that.

"What happened to you?"

He touched the wound. "Nothing of consequence."

"Liar." The Mahdfel healed quickly. Anything that left a gash was of consequence.

"A misstep in the training arena. It won't happen again." His voice was firm and decided. Whatever happened, whatever kept him away from her, would not happen again.

"You're late." Mercy tried to sit up and winced, from both the throbbing pain in her abdomen and the neediness in her words. She hated how she clung to Paax for support, how alone she felt when he wasn't there, but, dang it, a woman needs her husband when she's in labor. She refused to feel guilty for wanting her husband to hold her hand when she needed him most. If anything, she should be forcing an apology from him for leaving her high and dry. The only person who'd held her hand was Dorothy.

And shouldn't a proper mother's first concern be for her baby? Shame flowed through her because the first words out of her mouth wasn't for the welfare of the baby but because her husband didn't hold her hand and hurt her feelings. Some mother she was going to be.

"I came as soon as I could." He crouched down next to the bed and pressed his forehead to hers. She closed her eyes instinctively, savoring the contact.

"I needed you," she said, voice raspy and dry. She wanted to keep accusation from her voice but it was a struggle just to form words.

"Here." Paax pressed an ice chip to her lips. It melted on contact, soothing her parched mouth. She motioned for more.

A flurry of activity broke out in the room. The bed was adjusted to a sitting position, pillows propped behind her back, medication administered and a light, floating feeling disconnected her from the pain in her body. Everyone's attention was centered on her but no one actually spoke to her. The haze of anesthesia wore off and the fog of confusion left her mind. The medics checked her vitals and finally—finally—someone thought to inform her that the surgery was a success.

"The baby?"

"Healthy. Perfect warriors the pair of them," Paax said, chest swelling with pride.

Pieces clicked into place. Mercy remembered perfectly the curious light headed sensation of her chest being squeezed, and then Kalen barking out orders that the twins' heart rates were dropping.

"Twins," she said.

"Can you believe our good fortune? Two sons." Paax straightened, speaking to someone over her head and completely ignoring her.

"You are very fortunate, sir," Kalen agreed.

A wide grin flashed white against the warm plum of Paax's complexion, the warlord thoroughly pleased with himself.

Somehow that was the thing to push her over. Not the being ignored by everyone in the room. Not her husband's absence during her labor when it took a terrifying turn. Heck, not even the way her doctor conveniently forgot to tell her that she carried twins—but her husband apparently knew.

No, it was the way Paax puffed out his chest with that self-satisfied grin, like he was the one to carry two babies in his body. Or to suffer through sleepless nights, mood swings, swollen ankles, back pain, tender nipples, twice a day medical appointments and never had a moment to himself because a flotilla of warriors had to follow him everywhere. She did all the work and he took all the credit. Right now all she wanted was to hold the product of that work—nine months and change—in her arms and count his fingers and toes and kiss his little nose.

Noses.

Twins.

That explained all the punching and kicking. Four restless little feet had her convinced the kid was an acrobat. Turns out it was two acrobats.

A hand on his sleeve caught Paax's attention. "I'd like to hold my sons now. And you two can also explain why no one thought fit to inform me that I carried twins," she said when her husband bent his neck towards her.

She sounded calm, which was important because she did not feel calm. Far from it. If she'd had the energy and something handy, she'd be throwing stuff at the walls and shouting at the top of her lungs. She still might if a certain pair of aliens didn't get their purple butts in gear and let her hold her babies.

Forget them. She'd climb out of this bed and do it herself.

"What are you doing, female?" Kalen asked, alarmed.

"You're too slow. I'm going to find my babies." Her legs moved just fine, albeit slowly. Her entire middle, stiff and unwieldy, was the problem. Numbness wrapped around her abdomen, masking pain. It was like she wasn't even connected to her body or she was driving a car from the passenger side seat. She could almost reach the pedals but not quite. "What did you do to me?"

"Remain in bed," Kalen snapped.

Mercy lifted her chin and planted a foot on the floor. Screw him.

"You had major surgery," he added, voice softening. Skilled hands lifted her legs and put her back in the bad, pressing her shoulders down gently. "We cut through muscle here." His hands moved, indicating a vertical line right through her belly button.

Mercy lifted up the gown. An angry red line bisected her still round belly.

The incision looked painful. She poked it with her index finger. Nothing. "Why doesn't it hurt?"

"Medication and the pure raw talent of your medic," Kalen said without a trace of humility.

"Looks a little large. Did you have to butcher me?"

"Time was a factor," he said with a frown. "I needed to extract both your sons quickly."

With no regard to bikini season, apparently. She poked at the incision again.

Paax gently knocked her hand away. "Let it heal, little star."

"I'm going to have a scar."

Kalen huffed. "That will fade in time and with reparative cream. Human skin is too soft. That is not my fault. It will also not be my fault if you injure yourself running about like a stubborn female before you've had sufficient time to recover."

Bed bound. Fantastic. Just what a mother of twins needed to hear. "I wasn't going to run," she said under her breath.

Paax picked up her hand and crouched at her bedside. "Medication will block pain, which may mislead you to believing you are well enough to go about as you please, but this is a lie. Our technology is advanced and you are healing faster than an unassisted Terran, but there are limits. You must rest."

That voice. Deep and authoritative, it was a voice accustomed to being obeyed. Tired and numbed, her body—the traitor—responded to it as it wrapped around her, reassuring her of her place in the universe and made her feel safe. It was so hard to hold onto her anger when he had a voice like that.

"I need to hold my sons, Paax."

He nodded and motioned to a medic in the room. Done.

"How long will I be stuck in bed?"

"A day," her husband said. "The incision is already closed and healing but you must rest or it could reopen."

Mercy sank back into the pillows. A day wasn't so bad. "Okay, then let's talk about how neither of you two knuckleheads thought to mention that I was having twins."

Kalen and Paax exchanged a look.

Oh heck no.

The suspicion that they were holding something back from her gnawed at the back of her mind for weeks but she wrote it off as being overly tired and stressed. That conspiratorial look confirmed all her paranoid thoughts.

"You knew! What did you think would happen when two babies popped out? That I'd be too tired to notice the surprise double babies or too emotional to care that my *doctor* and my *husband* kept this from me."

"Little star—" Paax laid a hand on her shoulder but she shrugged him off.

"No, don't go distracting me with that sexy voice. I'm upset with you, Paax, and I have every reason to be. I have a right to make informed decisions about my care." Kalen opened his mouth to speak but Mercy cut him off. "Don't you dare say a thing. Just because you wear a white lab coat does not mean you get to make decisions about me *for* me. That goes for you, too, Paax."

He opened his mouth to speak.

Mercy held up the hand to a gesture to stop. Exhaustion rolled through her. She couldn't fight now, as much as she —they—needed to reach an understanding on why what they did was inconsiderate, demeaning and... and... just plain humiliating, like she was incapable of making decisions for herself about herself. So much in the universe was beyond her control and usually she went with the flow without complaint. She had no say in the alien invasion that killed her father and changed Earth forever, no say in registering for the Draft and no say in who she married. She sure as a heck would have a say in what happened to her own body.

"I'm tired, Paax. We'll talk about this tomorrow. Right now I want to hold my sons. Please."

"I am not tired," Kalen said, "and I need to inform you that withholding information of the twins was done to minimize your risk."

Sure, now he wanted to inform her.

Meridan arrived with a swaddled pink infant in either arm. "Not now, sweetie," she said, brushing past her mate. The alien doctor frowned, looked as if he was about to put his foot in his mouth but thought better of it. Good.

Mercy forgot all her worries, anger, pain, odd numbness and exhaustion. Her world centered on those two babies and their dusky pink complexions. She reached for them.

Meridan settled one in Mercy's left arm. Entranced by chubby cheeks and rosy lips, she gentle brushed a finger across his forehead. He had a shock of dark hair.

Nothing should be that cute.

Her son. He did not have a name, yet, but she knew it in her heart. Speaking it aloud would have to wait for the Naming Ceremony.

She placed a kiss on his forehead and murmured, "I know who you are."

The bed shifted as Paax sat next to her.

The second baby was placed in her right arm. "I know your name," she said with a kiss to his soft, downy head. He smelled so good.

He opened his vivid blue eyes and squalled, cheeks turning a darker pink.

"I think he's hungry, mama," Meridan said.

"Oh. How do I?"

The nurse helped her arrange the baby for breastfeeding and Paax held the sleeping infant. "Is feeding safe with the meds I'm on?" she asked.

"Absolutely."

"What about—" Mercy glanced over to the son Paax held.

"We'll feed sleeping beauty when he wakes. Double breast feeding is an advanced move. Let's just try one-on-one for now."

The baby cried again. Her breast ached in response. She held him to her chest and he burrowed his face against the offered breast. A warm, wet mouth clamped down on her nipple, rough at first but easing up. Pressure released in her chest. She didn't realize how heavy and swollen she was until the pressure eased.

"Okay, some basics," Meridan said. "First, not everyone can or likes to breastfeed. Some babies are biters. Some will chew your nipples up like it's bubble gum. Mahdfel milk teeth come in early and they're sharp. There's no shame in bottle feeding."

Bubble gum. That was horrifying to picture.

"Second, a human baby consumes a staggering amount of calories. Mahdfel babies even more so. You will probably not be able to produce enough milk for twins, so don't hesitate to supplement with formula."

The nurse's voice drifted into the general background. Mercy paid no attention. She only had eyes for the tiny, perfect being in her arms. Look at that skin, so smooth and flawless and soft. So soft. She counted ten fingers, perfect and grasping. Ten toes on two perfect feet. Two eyes. Two ears. She ran a finger over the top of his skull, careful of the soft spot and searched for horn buds. Two little protrusions waited just below the surface.

"Does that make sense?" Meridan asked.

"Sure," she said absently. "When will his horns come in?" Mercy looked towards Paax.

"Soon."

Full, the baby ceased feeding but did not let go of the nipple. Mercy rubbed his back, amazed at the size of him. "I guess I should be thankful they didn't grow in utero." Ouch.

"Ready to switch?"

Mercy nodded, accepting the other baby. He was slower to wake but happily accepted the nipple.

"This one feels… different," she said.

"Different good or bad?"

"I'm not sure. It doesn't hurt."

"Hmm." Meridan double checked the angle and connection, rubbing the baby's back when he complained. "Sometimes milk production isn't equal. Also, he's developing his technique."

That made her laugh, shaking the soft flesh of her belly. She tensed, waiting for pain but only found numbness. "A signature move. I guess that's one way to tell them apart."

Paax

EXHAUSTION FINALLY OVERCAME HIS MATE. She fought it, insisting on feeding their sons and holding them until they went to sleep, but eventually her eyes grew heavy. Her head lolled on his shoulder. The sounds of the medical bay filtered into their room. He would rather be in their quarters, in their own bed, but not even the warlord could defy the orders from the head of medicine. Mercy's health and welfare came first, always.

Carefully, Paax extracted himself from the bed and covered her with a blanket.

The star pendant weighed heavily in his pocket. His plans to present the jewel to his mate had vanished when she woke and there hadn't been to be an appropriate moment since then.

How about now?

He paused at the door to the room. The moment was private but he was reluctant to wake Mercy. Her rest was precious and there would be little of it in the coming weeks.

No, he decided. The gift of the pendant could wait.

In medical, Paax found Kalen. "Is there a problem, Warlord?"

"I want your report."

The medic nodded and consulted his data tablet. Paax did not know the male well, mistrusted his youth, but had no doubt that Kalen was the most talented medic in the Mahdfel military.

"Your sons are healthy and robust."

"No defects?"

"Are defects to be expected?"

Paax made a non-committal noise. He'd given himself a dose of the same compound that changed his brother, albeit a smaller dose. Worries nagged him. He knew how the experimental serum affected him but he did not know how it might affect the genes he would pass to his sons.

Kalen handed the tablet to Paax. "By every measure, they are ordinary."

"Ordinary. Not exceptional?"

"Did you want an honest report, warlord, or for me to kiss your ass?"

Another noncommittal noise. The most talented Mahdfel medic had the ego and audacity to match his extraordinary talent.

"Exceptionally ordinary, then," Kalen said.

"They are small."

"They are within the acceptable weight range. Terrans are small and your sons will grow."

His little star was, well, little. Kalen did not have to remind him that Terrans were diminutive.

"And my mate?"

"Recovering well. It was a stroke of luck that she was in medical when the twins went into distress."

A warning rumbled in his throat. His sons' survival, his mate's life, should not have been preserved by *luck*.

"Terrans are surprisingly strong for beings so small," Kalen said quickly. "As is your mate, in particular. I'm sure we would be having this same debriefing if she had not been in medical when the twins went into fetal distress."

Paax doubted that. "The length of her recovery?"

"Two days for the acute effects of surgery but she needs to rest for at least a week. Medication and the hormones Terran females produce will mask pain. She may push herself too hard too quickly and injure herself. A week of bed rest would be optimal but I suspect she will protest. No lifting. No straining muscles."

"And the future?"

"I see no reason why she would not be able to have more children."

"Twins?" Images of his mother flashed through his mind.

Kalen was slow to respond, which said everything Paax needed to know, really. To have another set of twins would be too risky for his mate. Even with constant medical care, the best medical care known to Mahdfel, it would be too risky.

"What are our options?"

"We control her fertility and implant with a single embryo when ready."

Paax turned the suggestion over in his mind. His twins developed from a single embryo splitting, not from two ova being fertilized. It was possible to discourage an embryo from splitting but would require some time in the genetics labs. "That is acceptable."

"Since we are on this issue," Kalen said, shoulder squared and poised for a fight. "Your female must not become pregnant before I can administer a birth control shot."

"Of course."

"And she needs time to heal. Completely."

Paax narrowed his eyes. Was this medic screwing up the courage to forbid him from having sex with his wife? "What do you take me for? Some beast that cannot control his cock long enough to allow his mate to heal after she whelped?"

"I believe you are a male who did not heed me the first time I gave medical orders regarding your mate. Her body suffered a great amount of stress. She needs to heal and recover. Her hormones are in flux. Terran females are susceptible to pregnancy in this stage and two such pregnancies, back to back, would be disastrous for your mate. Leave her alone until she is on birth control. Is that clear?"

Paax held the medic's gaze. He did not find defiance or opposition, only frankness. To the male's credit, he did not flinch or look away. "Understood," Paax said.

CHAPTER 8

Mercy

fter a thorough exam, Kalen declared Mercy and the twins "within acceptable limits" and were allowed to go home.

Home was a never-ending rotation of feeding, changing diapers and naps. Dorothy, proud grandma that she was, helped. Feeding, however, was directly on Mercy. Paax stayed closed by and demanded to be initiated into the mysteries of burping babies.

She had no pain, which was something of a marvel. Mercy assumed she would have pain. After all, the medics sliced open her abdomen. There should be pain. Instead her muscles were stiff and her head felt as if she were in a fog, but that could be exhaustion. She grabbed sleep whenever she could, fifteen or twenty minutes at a time but the twins refused to sync their sleep cycle. It seemed as if one woke the moment the other fell asleep. And they always woke hungry, and crying out. Her breasts ached and leaked at the sound of their cries.

Voices woke Mercy this time. She recognized the deep timber of Paax and the slightly thin, distorted voice of another male. Warlord business, not baby business. She could go back to sleep but her bladder urged her out of bed.

Paax stood in the common room, talking to someone on the view screen. That was not unusual behavior for him and she learned to ignore the details of his position. She crept around the edges of the room to remain off camera and quiet. Normally she didn't care if another Mahdfel saw her come and go—this was her home, after all—but her hair was a matted mess and she hadn't showered in two days. Momma had her pride.

"I understand congratulations are in order," the unknown male said. "You are fortunate to have such a pretty, fertile mate."

Mercy paused. Did the male see her after all? Was that comment sarcastic? No, the Mahdfel didn't do sarcasm. Literal and concrete they did, not snark.

"Two sons are a gift from the universe. To have a brother is, as you know, precious."

"What do you want, Antomas?"

"My brother alive and well but since that's not in the stars, how about the rest of his body?"

On the screen, a male so pale he was nearly grey held up a severed head by the hair. Eyes vacant, the head stared out of the screen. Mercy's stomached rolled and she stuffed a fist in her mouth to prevent herself from gagging.

"Antu challenged his warlord. He knew the consequences," Paax said, unphased.

"I don't like you," the male said.

"You don't have to."

"Everyone knows you seized the warlord's position through trickery and deceit."

"Guile. It's called guile."

Paax's flippant attitude enraged the male, causing him to toss the severed head to the floor and a roar. "It is an outrage that you command the largest Sangrin clan! And it is unfathomable that an honorless scientist defeated a warlord such as Omas Nawk. And it is unbearable that you defeated my brother. I will have my vengeance."

Paax displayed no reaction to the male's temper tantrum. "Would it ease your suffering to know that I had no preparation or plan in place for your brother's ill-advised challenge? Does that make it bearable?"

The connection broke down into unintelligible shouts. Chest heaving, staring directly into the screen, the male said, "I will take all you cherish, Paax Nawk. I will have your clan. I will have the *Judgment* and she will flourish under a strong warlord."

"If you think that is what I cherish, you are as short-sighted as your brother."

"I will have your mate and raise your sons as my own."

This struck a nerve. Paax strode towards the screen. Even with one horn missing, he must have looked fierce because the male visibly flinched. "I met Antu in a fair contest because it is every warrior's right to challenge their warlord. You can either accept this or not, I will not lose sleep on the matter but no one will say that the battle was not just. If you seek vengeance, I will hunt you down. I will destroy your and your little clan. How many warriors do you command? Fifty? And if you so much as think about harming a hair on my mate's head, I will hunt down your blood relatives—cousins, uncles, their sons and even your mother's people—and eradicate your weak blood from the universe. Do we understand each other?"

Antomas breathed heavily, nostrils flaring. Finally, he nodded. "This is not over."

"It is for you." Paax disconnected the call.

He stood in silence, tension slowly draining from his shoulders and back. "I know you are there, little star."

Mercy came out of the shadows and into the light. "You said the cut was from sparring and of no consequence."

"I believe my exact words were a misstep in the training arena." And then he smiled.

Unbelievable.

Wore thin from exhaustion, everything came to a head: he was never around, kept information about her health from her, kept the twins secret from her—while they were inside her, even—and now this. "You think this is funny? I asked you what happened because I was concerned about you and you lied to me."

"I did not lie."

"Really? Because the conversation I heard tells me you were fighting a challenger while I was in the middle of giving birth to our children and then when I asked you how you were injured, you brushed it off as a misstep, like it was a sparring injury. How is that *not* a lie?"

"I was in the training arena when it happened. I simply did not expound on all the details." He reached for her but Mercy took a step back.

"Seriously? Lying through omission is still lying. I don't know why I should expect anything different from you, though. This is so fucking typical."

The curse word made him pause. Mercy never cursed. Good. Maybe he would take her seriously.

"You are tired and easily upset."

"Don't give me that line of bull. I am tired, Paax. Tired down to my bones and especially tired of you not involving me in decisions that affect our family." Mercy sank down onto the sofa, moving stiffly. On the low table was a cup of the sour fruit tea Paax preferred.

He lifted his chin and his back went rigid. "I refuse to have a conversation with you when you are like this."

"Like what? What am I like? Because you've never really had a conversation with me, period." A year married and in this moment her husband looked at her like she was a stranger.

"Emotional. Irrational."

"Yeah, Terrans, huh? They get their panties all in a bunch wanting to be treated with respect and like a person. So strange." Bitter sarcasm laced her words. "This is just like you deciding not to tell me about the twins."

"That was for your own good."

"My own good, right. Can you just try see my point of view? You took a decision away from me, like I'm a child." Mercy grabbed a pillow and wrapped her arms around it, seeking comfort from something, anything.

"Everything I have done has been to keep you safe."

Safe, that wonderful catch-all Paax used to explain away all his bad behaviors. He had to claim her immediately, to keep her safe. He had to challenge the warlord, to keep her safe. He surrounded her with a squad of warriors just to keep her safe. He kept her in the dark about her own pregnancy... to keep her safe.

She didn't feel like his wife. She felt like... she didn't know. Nothing as kind as being a wife.

Mercy fiddled with the pillow on her lap.

"Do you think I'm stupid?" Her voice wavered at the end of the question. The other brides that arrived on the *Judgment* were professional, skilled and so talented. They were nurses, engineers, computer programmers, school teachers, a chemist, a botanist and she was... nothing special.

Paax was a genius, a no-joke genius. He designed the genetic test that matched women to the Mahdfel, that matched *them*. And what did she do?

She worked in a vet's office back on Earth. She didn't do any of the complex procedures like draw blood. Mostly she cleaned up after the animals. She barely finished school. College was out of the question, not when she had to take care of her mother.

"How can you think that of me?"

"How can I not? You don't ask for my opinion. You don't ask for my input. You make decisions without me."

"A warlord makes decisions! I do not have the time to consult you about every detail in running this clan."

"I'm not talking about the warlord business." Mercy held out her hands parallel, like she held an invisible box filled with warlord business. She moved both hands to the left, setting down the box. "I'm talking about us." She moved her hands to the right, indicated another invisible box. "You make decisions that affect both of us. You kept information from me, like I'm a child or you think I couldn't possibly understand, like you don't respect me."

"I have never said those words."

"You don't have to say the words! Actions speak loud enough!" She gestured widely with one hand and knocked over the cup of tea. The plastic material bounced on the floor and a bot rolled out, cleaning up the spill. She wanted to throw something, to bust some dished but all the cups were plastic and bots did all the cleaning. The brutal efficiency took away all the cathartic joy of a proper tantrum.

Paax retrieved the cup and placed it on the table. The scolding look he gave her was worse than anything he could have said. If she didn't want to be treated like a child, she shouldn't act like one.

Mercy rubbed the bridge of her nose. "Look, I'm sorry I yelled. That's not productive."

"No one is perfect."

She raised an eyebrow. Now was not the time for Paax to get a sassy attitude. "On Earth we have a few words to mean the person we married: wife, husband, spouse and partner."

"I am familiar with these titles."

"I don't feel like your partner, Paax. We don't talk. We don't work together. We don't make decisions together."

"We talk. We're talking now."

They were fighting now but Mercy didn't want to lose her train of thought to correct him. "You buy me toys. You give me playthings. You give me scraps of your attention. I'm not your partner, Paax. I'm a pet."

"You are no such thing. You are my mate." He took her roughly in his arms and pulled to his chest, holding her here as if to placate her.

Mercy didn't struggle. There was no point. He was solid muscle and there was no escaping his embrace until he released her. Why couldn't he admit that what he did was crappy? Why did he always have to be justified? Even if keeping her in the dark was—somehow—justified, he could at least acknowledge her hurt emotions.

A cry pierced the air. Her breasts ached in response. Feeding time.

"I have to go," she said and Paax released her. "We're not done discussing this."

"There is more?"

"Yes, there's more! You don't know the first thing about me."

"I know enough."

"If we were just starting out, sure, but we're a year into this and can you name my favorite Beatle?"

His brow furrowed. "Coleoptera? You make no sense."

"They were human musicians and George Harrison, thanks for asking. Honestly, Paax, this is the part of the argument where you should be asking me questions to show some interest. What's my favorite color? Song? Food?"

Paax was silent, proving her point. They were strangers.

The wail increased in pitch. Her little man was hungry and impatient. "Let me feed him and we can talk."

When Mercy came back to the common room, baby nestled against her chest, she found the space empty. Paax was gone. She lowered herself to the sofa, cradling her son as he fed. Light gleamed off something on the low table, catching her attention.

She picked up a crystal starburst pendant, sans chain. Amethyst colored stones formed the tips of the star. It was another lovely and ultimately empty trinket. She'd add it to the pile.

Paax

FURY PROPELLED PAAX FORWARD. The training bots took the brunt of his frustration. As he pounded the machine, denting the frame, disabling it and summoning a replacement, the other warriors gave him a wide berth. Exercise was a good outlet but none of them wanted to be the one to absorb their warlord's blows. Better a few broken training bots than broken limbs.

He growled in annoyance. His warriors should not be so soft to avoid a few broken bones and injuries. Those could be healed easily enough, unlike his mate's heart.

His mate was unhappy and he did not understand the reason. Everything he had done was done with her comfort and safety in mind. Everything.

A flurry of blows landed on the training bot. It stumbled under the pummeling before regaining its footing and blocked Paax's sword. Unfortunately it did not block the warhammer aimed for its head. The metal casing crumpled with impact. Another bot disabled.

Unacceptable. He needed better equipment.

Had he not become warlord to spare her from Omas' cruelty? He challenged his brother for her, his *twin*... The void in his soul once occupied by his twin never healed. He lived with the sensation of being incomplete for her.

Only her.

His chest heaved with exertion.

The problem she described required more than assigning another warrior to her guard, more than finding a botanist to grow flowers to decorate their apartment, and more than having a chef prepare her meals, more than bringing her Terran family to her.

He had no idea how to fix this.

He knew his wife intimately on a physical level but they remained strangers intellectually.

Sharing his thought process had never been his strength. He often leapt ahead of others and forgot to explain his leaps. As a geneticist he brought results and no one questioned his methodology. He brought Mercy results. He changed so much of his world for her, to carve out a peaceful existence for their family, and she failed to recognize his actions for the acts of devotion that they were. He failed to explain himself.

Had his parents experienced this? Neither were around to ask and Paax only had his foggy memories to guide him.

His mother was always pregnant, usually with twins. He remembered that clearly. He remembered her hugs and her soft, round belly. He remembered times when she was sick in the mornings and then times when she went to medical. Why, he could not say exactly, but he knew that he and Omas were his parents' only surviving children. He could only speculate that she lost all the others.

It had to wear on his mother and his father. Did the need for solace and comfort bring them together? Or did repeated loss build a wall of silence between them?

All he wanted was to spare his mate the pain his mother endured.

Good intentions meant nothing if he didn't explain himself.

CHAPTER 9

Mercy

One Week Later

The thing about an argument is they take real commitment to keep alive. Without dedicated time and energy, the reason for the argument might not slip away but the feelings of betrayal diminish. After a week of feeding two hungry infants, changing diapers and sleeping at most than two hours at a stretch, Mercy was too exhausted to keep fighting.

Paax came and went but they didn't talk. Not really. They exchange updates about their children. Their interactions were polite with a chill of distance that did not help her feel better at all. She poured out her grief and frustration to her husband and what did he do? He left for a day. When he came back, he didn't address their argument. He acted as if nothing happened.

Mercy refused to act as if nothing happened.

She wasn't wrong to be upset. Her feelings were not just hormones and not just exhaustion. They were real. The problem was real. Her husband did not respect her or treat her like a partner.

She had no idea what to do, so she did the basics: feed the babies, change the babies, sleep, shower—yeah, that hadn't happened in three days—and remember to eat. Repeat.

The Naming Ceremony inched closer by the day but it was easy to forget herself in the daily routine of being a mom. To think she was worried about being a good mom–she'd laugh if she had the energy. Her own insecurities gnawed away, comparing herself to the other women on the *Judgment*. So many of them were professionals but Mercy had cared for her ill mother for years. If anyone was prepared to be a mother, it was her.

Mylomon arrived just as she put Axil and Drake down to sleep. She decided on the names Paax suggested—the good ones— and even had an idea who was who. Axil was far more demanding and more of a biter when it came to feeding. Drake was relaxed and had to be coaxed into nursing. She hoped he didn't grow into a fussy eater.

"Warlord's female—"

"Paax isn't here." He was spending more time in his ready room and she suspected that he slept there. He certainly wasn't sleeping in their bed.

"I came to speak with you." His tone was precise, overly formal and made her suspicious.

"What do you want?"

He held out a dark fist and opened it, palm up. A crystal bead rested in the palm of his hand, so small and delicate in his huge paw. He looked at her expectantly. When she didn't react, he shook his hand as if encouraging her to take the bead.

"I don't know what you want."

"This is for you."

"I really don't know what you mean."

Mylomon sighed, his massive shoulders heaving. "You dislike me so much that you refuse my gift?"

"You didn't exactly make a great first impression but what are you talking about?"

"Paax did not explain." Not a question, a statement. Paax explained nothing. Typical.

"Maybe you can explain it to me."

"This," he said, holding the bead up so that the light caught in its belly, "is tradition. A new father presents his mate with a token, a pendant or stone, in appreciation for all that she has given him."

Mercy nodded. Gifts of jewelry she understood.

"It is good luck for the unmated and childless males to give smaller tokens to the new mother, so that her fortune and fertility may reflect back on them."

Her hand sought the crystal and amethyst pendant in the robe pocket. "He never mentioned this."

"Then I am honored to give you the first token. Please accept."

"So that Daisy will get pregnant?"

His eyes gleamed. "So that she will remain healthy and thrive."

"Thank you, I'm touched." She accepted the bead. A starburst pattern was carved into the surface and a small hole bored through the center, the perfect width for a chain. "This is lovely."

"And I apologize for my first impression." He bowed his head slightly, conveying sincerity.

"You stabbed me."

"I followed orders."

"Those orders sucked."

"Yes, but it was necessary. Necessity is often unpleasant."

Mercy narrowed her eyes. "You trying to imply something?"

A grin broke across his face. She fought the urge to recoil back because, dang it, he was a predator barring his teeth and it was terrifying. "If I have something to say, I say it directly."

"That's not what Daisy says. She says you're all about those long silences filled with meaningful looks and sighs."

"I do not sigh." His head tilted, listening to something only he could hear. "You should discuss pregnancy risks with Meridan."

Mercy rolled the bead in her hand. "That traitor? She could have told me about the twins but didn't, so I don't think so."

"I followed the standard protocol, so that makes me a traitor?" Meridan set her bag on the table near the entryway.

Mercy blushed. She would have never criticized the nurse had she known Meridan was in the room. Not in the room was a different, criticism-filled, story. "I thought my check-ups were over."

"Yeah, well, my darling husband is working my last nerve today, so I thought I'd make a house call," Meridan said, opening her bag. "How are you feeling?"

"Tired."

Mylomon bowed and showed himself out.

Meridan waved a scanner over Mercy. "Any pain? Nausea?"

Mercy shook her head. "Physically I feel good. Surprisingly good."

The nurse examined the incision and pressed down on her abdomen before instructing Mercy to lay down. She pressed down on her belly again before having her roll over and repeat the motion on her back. "And emotionally?"

"If you're trying to ask if I'm still pissed, you know the answer to that."

Meridan patted her on the shoulder, indicating that she could sit up. "I'm a hypocrite, I know."

"You knew I was having twins the entire time and you didn't tell me. Not once. You knew Kalen and Paax were keeping it from me and you didn't lose a bit of sleep, did you?"

"Don't get too comfortable on your high horse."

Mercy snorted. Her high horse was *very* comfortable.

"You are in the very lucky minority of women who have delivered surviving twins," Meridan said, voice laced with authority. "Half of all twin pregnancies will lose one baby; 25% lose both babies. And it's well documented that stress, even a small amount of stress, has drastic impacts on the mother's health. And if we told you? You'd want to know those statistics, wouldn't rest until we told you, and those numbers are pretty darn grim. So we decided to not tell you, to avoid stress during pregnancy and to minimize complications."

Minimize complications. Mercy hated how clinical that sounded, how cold. "If the worst happened, if I lost one of my sons... would you have even told me?"

Meridan fiddled with the instrument in her hand before raising her eyes to meet Mercy's gaze. "Its standard procedure to let the mate decide how much information is disclosed."

"So no." Paax already said he wouldn't tell her, in a

misguided effort to shield her from heartbreak. He didn't see the issue and Meridan actually *defended* their crummy decision. "It's so—"

"Demeaning? Belittling? Disenfranchising?"

Mercy nodded.

"The alternative is heartbreaking."

"What happens if I have twins again?"

"Survival odds decrease."

Mercy rubbed the spot between her eyes. "How is that even possible? And how is it that everyone seems to think that I should be *grateful* that I was lied to for nine months."

Meridan did not answer, instead packing away her instrument. "You're recovering nicely. Try to sleep more."

"Yeah, sure." She slept when she could. At least Axil and Drake were on the same sleep cycle now but that had its problems. Two hungry babies awake and demanding to nurse made for some interesting juggling. "What I need is another set of arms."

"Can I examine the babies now?"

Meridan performed her check on the sleeping infants. Either they were deep sleepers or Meridan had a light touch because Axil and Drake slept through the entire examination.

"Good weight. Good color. Strong vitals. How is their appetites?"

"Voracious."

"And bowel movements?"

"Disgusting."

She snickered. "I thought you weren't supposed to be grossed out when it's your own kid."

Two times the diapers took away cuteness and multiplied the gross. Mercy paused. "I can't get pregnant again, can I? Nursing stops that?"

"You absolutely can get pregnant again, but it's probably way too soon to think about sex. You need to heal."

She couldn't roll her eyes hard enough. She needed to get her husband in the same room and talk to him before she'd consider sex. Even so, she wasn't ready for another baby.

"I have patient confidentiality with you, right?"

"Yes. Anything you say is confidential and no one need know."

"Not even the head of medicine?"

Meridan paused before answering. "If it is vital to your health or safety, I am obligated to report that."

"And you can't tell anyone?"

"Your medical information is confidential," Meridan said.

Mercy nodded, believing that the nurse took her profession seriously and would not gossip with her husband about their conversation. "It's not that I don't want more kids. I do, but I'm not ready. I don't want—"

The nurse nodded and rooted in her bag, withdrawing a canister. "Birth control is a standard recommendation after pregnancy. Your body suffered a great deal of stress and needs time to recover before going through that stress again."

"I just need to sleep." And shower. And brush her hair.

Meridan loaded the canister into a hypospray and pressed it against Mercy's arm. She felt the slightest pinch. "This will last for a year. It can be neutralized with another injection but I caution against that. A year is a good break between batches. You'll still get wellness checks, too."

Mercy rubbed her arm, barely listening. "Thank you."

Paax

THERE WAS ALWAYS some issue or problem to command a warlord's attention. Paax kept himself busy and found plenty of reasons to remain in his ready room and not return to his shared quarters with his mate. The ship's computer monitored Mercy and sent him notifications when she was asleep. That was when he returned home to hold his sons and tell them of the great deeds of his father and his father's father. They barely listened and were far more interested in tugging on his lips and hair. The strength in their grip pleased him. They were small for Mahdfel infants but they were mighty.

Paax had always had trouble communicating his thoughts to others. He thought faster, such was his genius, often made leaps, and grew frustrated waiting for others to catch up, such was his ego. He worked best directing a team where the males followed his orders and did not question him. They understood that Paax had thoroughly thought out the problem and trusted that his method was best. That was how his lab worked when he served as a geneticist. That was how the *Judgment* worked when he became warlord.

To have his mate doubt him, to have to explain every decision when he made countless decisions daily…

He should apologize. He needed to apologize, but not just yet.

He investigated the musicians Mercy claimed to admire and listened to their entire catalogue. Terran music was not disagreeable but the rhythmic melodies were an acquired taste. After the first dozen hours, he found his foot keeping that alien rhythm.

The insect musicians grew on him.

The *Judgment* was ready to enter the Gate. The journey through the Gate would take an hour. For a vessel the size of the battle cruiser, passengers would not notice the hour in flux. They didn't even need to use a safety harness. It also meant that care of the *Judgment* rested solely with the navigator for the next hour and there was nothing for Paax to do but pace and unnerve Darian.

He decided to utilize the downtime and consume a meal.

Food had been reduced to barebones sustenance. He drew no pleasure from food, not with his mate upset.

In the cafeteria he found his mate's mother preparing a tray.

Dorothy looked up, surprise registering on her face. "Haven't seen you around lately," she said.

"I have many duties that require my attention."

He watched as she spread a legume paste on a bagel. He found the paste too sweet but knew his mate savored it. Dorothy noticed him watching. "Mercy has been trying to come down for breakfast for an hour now so I decided to bring it to her."

"She prefers oatmeal and honey for the morning meal." It baffled him how a plain grain could satisfy her and keep her from hunger but she insisted.

"Unless someone is there to spoon-feed her, she's limited to what she can eat with one hand." She picked up an orange globe and gestured with it.

Shame flooded Paax. He should be the one to feed his mate. She should not struggle on her own. Only his pride kept him from her side.

It boiled down to pride. He might be bad at explaining his reasoning and logic but his pride smarted when his mate did not accept that he had her best intentions in mind. She consumed his thoughts and directed his every action. How could she doubt him?

Because he avoided her when she needed him, like an honorless dog.

Paax plucked an orange globe off the tray and bit into it. Acrid bitterness flooded his mouth and he spit out the offending fruit. "Terrans eat this?"

"We don't eat the rind," Dorothy said. She demonstrated on a second orange how to peel the fruit. "This is the first harvest from our very own orange trees."

"This grew on the *Judgment*?" He peeled his orange, using his nails to separate the bitter rind from the fruit. He was imprecise and punctured the fruit, juice leaking down his hands.

"When I was a little girl," Dorothy said, "oranges were commonplace. Every grocery store had them; stacks and stacks. You bought them pounds at a time and they were cheap. During the invasion, they vanished, like a lot of stuff. The groves were all destroyed in Florida and California, I heard. They only started showing up again in stores a few years ago."

Paax said nothing as his mate's mother rambled. He could not afford to offend both females.

"We had orange *flavoring* and artificial juice pumped full of vitamin C but not the real thing. Do you know this will be the first real orange Mercy's had since she was a kid? Sometimes I can't believe the way the world changed."

Paax unpeeled the fruit and discovered that it had segments. He popped a segment in his mouth, savoring the acidity and sweetness. "What is this Terran fruit? I approve."

"An orange."

His brows furrowed. "My translator must not be working properly. That is a color."

"It is also the name of the fruit. This is a navel orange."

Terrans did enjoy words that had multiple meanings, almost as if they relished confusing their alien allies. He had interacted with enough to Terrans to believe this to be true.

"I should get back. She's waiting," Dorothy said, standing.

Paax placed a hand on the tray. "I will feed my mate, but first, please, I have three questions."

Dorothy sat back down.

"What is my mate's favorite color?"

"Aquamarine. She wears it often enough."

Paax nodded, turning this information over in his mind. He would know the information she demanded if he were observant. "And her favorite food is… chocolate?"

"Obviously. Is there a point to this?"

"One more. What is her favorite song?"

Dorothy glanced over her shoulder, towards the kitchen. "*Here Comes the Sun*. Charles use to sing… He sang it to Mercy during air raids." She sighed. "I haven't thought about that in years."

"Thank you for the information."

Back in his quarters, he found Braith standing guard at the door. Inside, his mate was in the cleansing room. Steam curled from under the door. His sons slept. Terran infants slept a lot, he learned, just not always in successive periods of time.

His sons slept together in one basket that Mercy insisted calling a bassinet. the word sounded like a Terran fish or a basket for fish. Soon they would outgrow the fish basket and require separate accommodations. For the moment they rested on their backs, holding hands.

"Always be good to each other," Paax said, his thumb brushing their downy hair. "You are brothers. You will need each other. Do not fight." It was the most important wisdom he could think to impart. He continued, "I had a twin once. We were inseparable. He was part of my soul. Even when we drifted apart, we were always together."

Omas had been his oldest and closest companion. For all his flaws, for all the cruelty that he would do as warlord, he had been a good friend and a better brother.

"Do you miss him?"

Mercy

PAAX STIFFENED at the sound of her voice. "Daily. It is like losing a limb but the sensation remains," he said.

"Or losing a horn?"

A hint of a smile played across his face. "Yes, just so."

"Sometimes I forget he was your brother," she said.

"Twin." His expression softened. "When I think of Omas, I do not remember the end. I remember him as we were, before our warrior training."

"When you were children. People change."

"Even as warlord," Paax said before a pause, as if searching for the correct words. "The cruelty only happened in the last years, after he lost his mate."

"Are you trying to convince me that the man who threatened to murder you and rape me was good and kind?" She could still feel how Omas had loomed above her, leering. Then leaned down and *sniffed* her hair. She had felt dirty after that.

"It would break me to lose you, little star. Losing Naomi did the same to Omas."

Mercy leaned against the doorframe. Paax stood over the bassinet. Axil or Drake, she wasn't sure, made a cranky noise. Even as he tried to convince her that that scariest person she ever met in real life deserved compassion, he stroked their son's back to sooth them back to sleep.

What kind of men did she want her sons to grow up to be? Ones with compassion? Ones who understood that the world was more than black and white, good guys and bad guys, and sometimes the ones who wronged you deserved empathy? Or men who held nothing tender in their hearts and only knew violence?

She'd lived a year now in the Mahdfel world and saw the violence first hand.

She wanted her sons to know compassion, too.

"Your brother made a terrible first impression. Like, the worst. Easily one of the top five worst human-alien first contacts."

He snorted, swallowing a laugh. She loved that sound. Mostly he made it when he read something inaccurate or when he was surprised but she loved it more when she inspired his near-laugh.

Shyness overcame Mercy. Wet hair clung to her and dripped down her back. The silk robe was barely tied. She adjusted the front and tightened the belt.

His eyes tracked her movements. "I brought your morning meal."

"Thank the stars, I'm starving."

A plate with a bagel and peanut butter and an already peeled orange waited for her in the common room. She sat curled up on the sofa and pulled the plate to her lap.

"Your mobility has improved," Paax observed.

"If that's your idea of an apology—" She sighed. "I'm sorry. I told myself that I wouldn't pick a fight the next time I saw you, so let me try again. Yes. I'm able to move pretty well now. I can even get in and out of a chair all on my own." She picked up an orange segment, closed her eyes and breathed deep the scent before popping it in her mouth. "Oh, that's so good. I haven't had a real orange in ages."

"Since the invasion."

Her eyes opened in surprise. "That's right."

"Chocolate, aquamarine and *Here Comes the Sun*."

She laughed. "Did you make a list?"

"You asked me to answer. I researched."

"For a week? I need you here, Paax."

His head nodded. "Now I am the one who must apologize. I have wronged you, little star, and it is difficult for me to know how to change."

"But you understand the problem, right?"

He sat on the sofa next to her. His arm went around her shoulder and she curled next his warm body. It felt so good to snuggle, to be safe in his arms and share in his strength. She didn't want to fight but she didn't want to be a doormat, either. She loved him too much to let him walk all over her.

"I love you, you know," she said.

"And I love you," he said. "You consume my thoughts, my actions."

"So why is this so hard?" They loved each other. Love conquered all, right?

"Because I am old and set in my ways. I have never had to explain my actions before."

"Not so old," Mercy murmured.

"But you agree about being set in my ways?"

"Try explaining your actions. I'm ready to listen."

Paax reached over and handed her the plate. She nibbled on the bagel while he collected his thoughts.

"My mother lost many children," he said. "That is the short version. Omas and I were our parents only surviving birth."

"Twins."

"Yes, which is rare."

"Meridan threw a bunch of statistics at me."

"As a child, I was too young to understand how dangerous it was for my mother to have so many pregnancies, how it wore her body down, but I saw the heartbreak."

"That had to be hard on your parents." She could easily picture her heartbreak if she lost one or, stars forbid, both of her babies. Her heart hurt just thinking about it.

"When I was older, I realized that my parents were not a good genetic match. This may have been the problem. So I made the test." The genetic test that matched human women to Mahdfel warriors; the test that matched them.

"Just like that."

He shrugged. "Do you want my story or do you want false modesty?"

"Wow," she said with a reluctant smile. "How do you manage with your head that big?"

"My head is average," he said with seriousness, like she was missing the point.

"I mean, can you wear a hat? Get a good night's sleep on our tiny pillows? Can you even stand up? The weight has to be enormous."

"You are teasing me."

"I am," she said, satisfaction soaking into her voice. "You're just so teaseable."

He grumbled under his breath but Mercy sensed he was pleased. Body language, relaxed and open, betrayed him. A hand on her back rubbed absently in a slow circle.

"So, after your humble brag, you…" she prompted.

He was slow to answer. "I wanted to spare you my mother's suffering."

"I'm not your mother."

"I am well aware."

"We're a strong match."

"Yes."

"But you worry."

"You consume my thoughts, I told you. Worry paralyzed me. The medic said the protocol was to keep the mother uninformed, to minimize emotional injury—"

"If Kalen thought it was a good idea, that's your first clue it's a bad one."

"I accepted his judgment as sound." He paused. "It was the wrong decision."

Mercy snorted. "I took the birth control shot."

She pulled back and studied his face for a reaction. "It's not that I don't want more babies, I do, just—"

"Kalen discussed birth control methods after your surgery."

"What did I just say about listening to Kalen?"

"And I said that I would discuss it with you when you were ready. We agreed that you required at least a year to recover completely."

Mercy settled back into him. "Thank you. That means a lot."

"You do not have to explain the actions you make to your own anatomy."

"That's awfully magnanimous of you."

"You are teasing me again."

"Damn straight I am." It felt so good to tease him. Things had been too serious between them.

His pulled her closer. She breathed in the warm, spicy scent of him. "I am not good at sharing my thought process. I am accustomed to giving orders."

"And being followed?"

He grunted. "I will try to explain my actions but know there may not be time to share every decision with you."

Her fingers twisted in the fabric of his shirt. "Just try for the stuff that impacts our family, okay?"

"Agreed."

"Good." Then, "I had an idea I wanted to discuss with you."

"Your timing is suspicious."

Mercy laughed. It felt so good to laugh. "It's actually something I talked over with Daisy way back when. I think we need a welcome committee for the new brides."

"And you would be this welcome committee?"

"Yes. Don't you think the warlord's wife should greet the new ladies? Give them a tour? Let them know they're not alone."

"Their mates should do that."

"But do they?"

He grunted. "A new bride arrived yesterday and her mate failed to take her to medical for the required examination."

"So there's a need. Think of it as human resources." Literally.

"Will you not be tired?"

"How often do we get new brides? Once a week? I can

handle it. Dorothy can babysit or I'll bring Axil and Drake along. Everyone loves cute babies."

His arms tightened around her. "Axil. Drake."

"Oh." She hadn't told she reached a decision on the names. "I settled on names."

"I had a good suggestion after all?"

She lifted her head to look at him. "You planted all those terrible names so I'd pick the ones you wanted."

"A necessary battle tactic." He kissed her forehead, softly.

"Or, you know, you could have just said what you wanted, like a normal person," she grumbled.

"I approve of your proposition," he said, changing subject. "It will help acclimatize the females to the clan and make all of us stronger. And we will learn how to work together on this, like partners. You will be a great helpmate, and the other males will be jealous."

"You say the sweetest things," she said as her skin prickled with a half-remembered story. "Where did you hear that phrase?"

"Eh?"

"Helpmate?"

"I don't follow."

"It's a phrase from an Earth creation story. Well, one creation story. We have lots."

"Humans like the sound of their own voice."

"Hush." She jabbed a finger into his stomach, which was like poking a stone wall for all the good it did. "Do you want to hear it?"

"Enlighten me."

"God created the universe. He—"

"Your god is male?"

"Are you going to listen or critique the story?"

Paax settled back into the cushions of the sofa. "Proceed."

"So God separated the light from the dark and the water from the land. He made life, plants and animals. Finally, he created man from the earth."

"A male."

"A human, but male. Adam. God was pleased with his creation but Adam was lonely, so God made him a mate."

Paax shifted, his interest peaked.

"Eve was made from Adam's rib."

"Not from the earth?"

"Look, that's the way the story goes. God made Eve and presented her to Adam and said, 'I have made you a help-mate' or something like that."

"What happened next?"

"Doesn't matter. It's an old story. Really old. Helpmate tickled my memory, that's all."

"It is a good story," he said with a nod of his head.

"Adam's mate was made for him, as you were made for me."

He really did say the sweetest things.

Three whistling notes alerted them to an incoming communication. Mercy's body tensed. Of course they couldn't have a peaceful moment to themselves. Paax's arm tightened around her, responding to her distress.

"This better be good," he growled.

"We just exited the Gate, sir," Mylomon said, his normally deep voice flattened through the comm. "I thought you might like to know about the Suhlik warship."

CHAPTER 10

Paax

Paax paced the length of the bridge. He had to set aside thoughts of his little star during the conflict. Concern and worry for her would paralyze him. He had to trust that Braith would follow orders.

The lighting went from normal blue and white light to a more aggressive red. The battle cruiser was on alert and the warriors prepared for conflict.

The situation was unacceptable.

No one knew the location of the *Judgment*. The council had only just realized that the battle cruiser was not where it was meant to be. The elderly members of the council sent demanding transmissions, as if they could intimidate or bully Paax into returning to the tranquil space around Sangrin.

Tranquil was tedious and his warriors needed something

more than a simple skirmish. They needed to bloody their fists in a pitched conflict. They needed a good, hard battle.

The council members were too old to remember what it was like to have fire in their blood, to burn with the need for battle. It was the Mahdfel purpose. They were made for battle. They needed to do more than patrol.

What was the point of a massive battle cruiser with cutting edge fire power and a complement of highly trained warriors if they just *patrolled?*

The *Judgment* emerged from a Gate to find a Suhlik warship waiting for them. For all the convenience of Gate technology, they were a huge security risk. Normally a Gate had a full complement of ships to secure the passage. A craft was most vulnerable in the moments after exiting a Gate as sensors and mapping functions updated.

This Gate, however, had been abandoned by it's Mahdfel sentry, for unknown reasons.

"Warlord," Darian said, "two more *colpor* class ships are approaching."

A *colpor* class ship held considerable firepower but not enough to rival the *Judgement*. Three against one significantly evened the odds.

Paax lead his clan right into a trap.

No one knew where they were headed. They had no orders. How could an ambush be waiting for them? Someone betrayed their flight plan.

Seeran would know who. Seeran always knew but the male was stuck on Earth until Vox resolved the business with his female. The *Judgment* would not have found itself in such unfavorable odds if Vox had not been matched. Females required a great deal to care for and protect, perhaps more than even a battle cruiser could provide, Paax admitted reluctantly. Omas might have been onto something when he forbade the warriors from taking mates.

No. That was not true. The battle cruiser's situation was entirely his fault. He did not defy a direct order from the council but he violated its spirit.

"How quickly can we access the Gate?"

"The Gate engine needs to recharge," Zadran said. Gates were powerful but slow and required a brief window between openings. "Fifteen minutes, minimum."

"Open that Gate. How long for the Suhliks ships to be in firing distance?"

"Ten," Zadran answered.

"All? Or just some."

"The lead ship will be within range in ten minutes. The second and third will arrive in twelve."

He needed five minutes. Or a way to convince the other Suhlik vessels to stay their distance. A firefight with his mate and children onboard was unacceptable on so many hellish levels.

"Orders, sir?" Darian asked.

"Hail the lead Suhlik ship." He wasn't in a position to negotiate. They didn't need to know that.

A golden scaled Suhlik male filled the view screen. His eyes went through the unsettling motions of blinking twice. "Paax Nawk. What an unexpected honor."

"I think it is entirely expected," he said. "I don't believe we've had the pleasure, captain—"

"Captain is good enough for the likes of you. I don't want my name on a dog's lips."

The Suhlik tried to anger Paax, hoping he'd make a rash and uncalculated move, exposing the *Judgment*. Fortunately for Paax he was able to be both infuriated and logical.

"This is Alva space," Paax said.

"The fringes, yes. And we both know that who controls what space really comes down to who has the most firepower."

Spoken like a true bandit. The Suhlik only took and always by force. "That would be me," Paax said. "The Gate is keying up for a new opening. Do you really want to wait and see what sails through?"

The Suhlik captain's top lip curled back, revealing wicked sharp teeth. "You bluff but even if you spoke true, reinforcement would not arrive in time. Every moment that ticks by is a moment your lumbering ship is closer to feeling the sting of my missiles."

"Just a sting?" The *Judgment* was huge, outfitted with the

latest in shielding technology and weaponry. Nimble it was not but it could absorb anything a single *colpor* ship would throw at it. "You better hail us when you start firing, otherwise we'll never know."

More teeth. Guttural shouts came off screen, demanding the uppity Mahdfel's blood. The captain ignored his crew and maintained eye contact with Paax. "With your mate onboard? I should congratulate you, Paax Nawk, for two live births. The twin mutation was a gene we never mastered. The fatality rate was too high to be advantageous."

The Suhlik knew about his mate and sons.

"I'm flattered you bother learning the details of a dog and his mate."

"You are a particularly talented dog, Paax Nawk."

Paax fought the urge to shiver as the Suhlik captain spoke his name, disgusted at the way the male rolled the vowel sounds in his mouth like a tasty morsel.

"Surrender yourself and I will spare your crew."

"Why would I do that?"

"Because my ships will overwhelm your slow and graceless ship and I will board and I will find your mate and I will take your sons."

Suhlik teleportation technology was superior to the Mahdfel tech. They were able to teleport in with pin-point precision. If the shield went down, they could very well teleport directly into his private quarters and seize Mercy.

More likely, they would slaughter her and take Axil and Drake, claiming them for a life of experimentation and torture.

"I'd sooner slit their throats than let you have them," Paax said.

The Suhlik captain nodded, unsurprised by this response. "Serve me, Paax Nawk. Use that brilliant brain for your Suhlik masters as you were designed to do."

"And you'll spare the crew?"

"Yes." The response came out as a long hiss, a forked tongue flicking over his lips.

"My crew can take care of themselves. You will spare all the mates and offspring on the ship. You will not board. You will not take anyone."

The response was slower this time. "Yes. Agreed."

"Let me think about it."

Paax motioned for the communication to be cut. "Time until they are within firing range?"

"You can't be serious," Mylomon said. "They will never honor such an agreement."

"Time." Paax knew better than to ignore his second's concerns. The Suhlik were liars and thieves and not to be trusted. Moreover, Mylomon had been stolen as a child and subjected to advanced *research*, if the abomination of science that was done to him could be considered research.

"Seven minutes," Darian answered. "You're not considering their offer, are you?" Paax gave the helmsman a sharp look. "Sir," he added.

"Mylomon—" Paax turned to his second in command.

"All pilots are activated. Our starfighters will be able to muster in two minutes." Clever male, anticipating his warlord's plan.

"Very good. And?"

"You want a raiding party. How many warriors would you deploy?"

"How many are ready?"

"All."

"All." Paax did not question Mylomon's statement. The male was not prone to exaggeration or fabrication.

"I want three boarding parties ready to depart the moment the pilots can give them coverage." At the moment the lead Suhlik ship was alone and would be alone and within the *Judgment* weaponry for two long, long minutes. That was enough time for the battle cruiser to keep it occupied and off the raiding shuttles. The starfighters added an extra level of coverage.

"Just three?"

"I want you on the fourth. Take our best warriors with you. Alert Kleve and Jolyon but leave Braith."

A slow grin spread over Mylomon's face. "And whose heart do you want as a trophy?"

"Not a heart. I want you to disable the lead ship. Any means necessary." His plan had a lot of moving parts but Mylomon seemed to grasp it. The *Judgment* would provide cover and harass the Suhlik ship while it was alone and vulnerable, allowing the raiding shuttles to board. Timing was crucial. If they were slow, the other two ships would arrive and they would be overwhelmed. No amount of volley from the *Judgment* would get them off the Suhlik ship again. They had to disable the ship, remove it from combat. The other ships would flee because Suhlik were cowards in their hearts and would never enter combat if the odds were not in their favor.

"Do you want it to self destruct?"

"Disabled. Do not destroy it. That's a newer model. I'm sure there's plenty we can salvage."

"Will you join the raiding party?"

Paax wanted to. The men needed to see their warlord in action and fight side by side as brothers. "I need to see the entire battle," he said with reluctance. Too much could go wrong. He needed to be here if the plan failed and the *Judgment* was boarded. He did not bluff when he said he would slit the throat of his family before letting them fall captive to the Suhlik. He had no doubt that Braith would follow that order but if Paax failed, he should be the one to wield the blade. He would do anything to protect his family and he would do the worst to spare them suffering as a Suhlik captive.

"And my pilot? You said take the best but Vox is on Earth."

"Then take an adequate but available pilot."

"Yes, sir. I'm sure Kheon will be thrilled to learn he is adequate and available." His voice remained deadpanned but a slight tug at the corner of his mouth revealed his mirth. For him, he positively bounced with pleasure. "We won't have long before the other Suhlik ships arrive."

"Then work fast."

Mercy

BRAITH REFUSED to say what the scary red lighting meant until they were in the safe room. He also refused to explain the presence of the safe room.

An undetectable panel slid back soundlessly in the floor, revealing a hatch and a ladder. There was no way she was going down that ladder carrying two babies. One, maybe, but she needed at least one hand to hold onto ladder. If she had a bit of warning she could have fashioned a papoose carrier or a sling. "Has this been here the whole time?"

Braith climbed down three rungs on the ladder. "We do not have time. I must secure you and the little warriors. Hand me one."

Mercy knelt at the opening and handed down Drake.

"Now the other."

Just as her feet touched the top rung, Dorothy ran into the room.

"Good, I'm not too late," she panted, face flush.

"What's happening, Mom?"

"There's a Suhlik warship but Paax didn't tell me much, just ordered me to the safe room with you. I got here as fast as I could."

Everyone knew about the safe room, apparently. She spent the last year living above it and never noticed. And now there was a Suhlik warship to worry about. She'd been through her fair share of skirmishes but never had the lights flashed red or had she been taken to a safe room.

Once down the ladder, Braith sealed the hatch. The safe room was a single room with a long bench along one wall and a bunk at the other. The walls and floor were constructed from a simple grey material. Hardly a resort. Harsh lightning did the stark space no favors. A quick inspection revealed a storage compartment under the bench with water and ration bars. A panel in the wall opened to a tiny cleansing room, barely tall and wide enough for her, let alone a full grown Mahdfel.

A cold chill ran over her in a moment of clarity. This safe room was never meant for a Mahdfel male. This was designed for a female, for her. How many other safe rooms were there in the *Judgment?* One under every floor or did her status as the warlord's wife give her such luxury? Were there secret hidey holes or compartments in the wall, big enough for a lone woman or a small child? She wanted to ask but she also didn't want to know the answer.

Mercy shivered and reached for one of the blankets folded on the bunk. She recognized the material as being the scratchy wool-like cloth Paax preferred. "Will you tell me what's going on?"

"The warlord did not inform me of the details," Braith said. He placed a chair at the foot of the ladder and sat. His sword was drawn and placed on his lap.

"That serious?"

"You are protected in this room. It is surrounded by impenetrable nanocarbon. The environment and power systems are self sustaining. No one will detect a power signature from the room."

"What about body heat? Wouldn't that show up on a scan?" Mercy cradled a sleeping Axil. Dorothy held Drake and rocked him gently, cooing soothing sounds.

"Impenetrable to all things, including scanners. A raider would have to know the room existed to detect it."

"And no one knows the room exists." She certainly didn't.

"Just us and the warlord. You are safe."

"We've had skirmishes with Suhlik warships before," Mercy said. "Why is it different now?"

Braith studied the edge of his blade.

"It's not just one warship, is it?"

He held the blade up to the light, gleaming a wicked blue.

"How many is it?"

He placed the blade back across his lap. "I will protect you if we are boarded, but be assured that no one could detect this room and if they did, it is impossible to open from the outside."

Braith's words did not make her feel better. If the worst happened, if the *Judgment* was board by the Suhlik, if they found the safe room, if they managed to open it, Braith would fight to the death.

Mercy turned to Dorothy. "You said Paax ordered you here. Did you overhear anything else?"

She shook her head. "Something about a raiding party but I was in the mess hall and everyone was talking at once."

"Tell me," Mercy said, returning her attention to Braith. "Paax called away Kleve and Jolyon. Why? Where is he sending them?"

Braith shifted in his seat. "I am not privy to the warlord's strategy."

"But you know something." He wouldn't look her in the eyes and she wouldn't let it go until he did.

"There are three Suhlik warships. If the warlord is sending a raiding party, he must mean to disable one of the ships and scatter the remains of the fleet or draw them away."

Mercy sucked in a breath. "And if the ship is not disabled?"

The electric blue edge of the sword hummed.

Mercy sank onto the bench, holding Axil. "This is it, isn't it?" Braith raised an eyebrow but said nothing. "I knew things were theoretically dangerous but I never really…" She didn't finish that sentiment. It was a dangerous universe and she was married to a man shadowed by conflict. Life would never be peaceful with a warlord. How many times would she be hustled into the safe room? How would she feel when Axil and Drake were grown and off to fight their own battles? Would they survive long enough to reach that point? Would Paax live long enough to see them grown? It was a vicious, heartless universe that guaranteed no one a happy ending.

"Sweetie," Dorothy said, adjusting the blanket that slipped from her shoulders.

No one told her not to worry or gave her false platitudes. She appreciated the silence.

"How will we know?" she asked Braith.

"Eh?"

"How will know if—" She paused and swallowed the lump in her throat. "How will we know to open the door?"

"The warlord will notify us," Braith said, confidence ringing in his voice. "Paax Nawk has never failed a challenge. He will not fail now."

CHAPTER 11

Paax

Paax split his attention between the point-of-view camera from Mylomon's raiding party, the larger view of his starfighters and their combat, and his chief engineer babbling in his ear. On the view screen, Kleve and Jolyon led a dozen warriors onto the Suhlik ship. They met with resistance but resistance was expected. Currently they were pinned at a corridor inter-section.

"We have a welcoming party," Jolyon said over the screen.

"Accept their surrender," Paax ordered. Suhlik rarely surrendered. If they could not win outright, they ran and if cornered, they fought to the death.

"Surrender doesn't seem to be on their agenda." Jolyon peered around a corner before efficiently using his rifle to pick off two incoming Suhlik foot soldiers. "I have to tell you, sir, this is fun. They're running around like a *cyw* without its head. It's beautiful."

"Now is not the time for humor," Mylomon said. He crossed quickly into the intersection, threw a dagger, and kept moving.

"You have something you need to be doing," Paax growled.

Another voice grabbed his attention. "You planning to turn my pretty ships into space junk or are you going to retrieve those disabled ships?" Rohn asked.

"Those are my ships, not yours, and they are not pretty," Paax said to the flight deck manager.

"Fine but your terrifyingly masculine ships are still space junk." The glee in the male's voice was unmistakable.

"Are you having fun? I don't want you having fun while my aesthetically unimportant and functional ships are being blown up."

"Well, I want an avocado but that's not going to happen. The ones out of the reconstructor are disgusting."

"A what?" Pilots were a strange breed. Too much time in deep space or not enough oxygen. Rohn didn't fly much anymore but the he was clearly still affected.

"A Terran food. It's squishy. Good for your horns."

"You can eat after the battle. Send drones. Prioritize those pilots with a heartbeat." There would be plenty of time to collect the dead but less time to save the living. "The last raiding ship made it. Those fighters still functioning should keep the Suhlik ship busy."

"Yes, sir."

"Computer, connect to Medical." The connection went through instantly. "Kalen, expect incoming casualties. The pilots." That would inform the medic to expect burn and blast damage, possible oxygen deprivation and maybe even frostbite if life support failed on a disabled ship. The Mahdfel were resilient and their exo-armor was substantial, but even they needed to breath.

"We're ready. How many am I expecting?"

"Rohn will have an accurate count for you." Paax cut the connection. "Darian, situation report."

"The lead ship is stationary but still has full power," the helmsman said.

"And the other two?"

"One is slowing. They could be planning to assist the lead ship or turn. I can't tell yet. The other is continuing on course to us."

One *colpor* class ship against the *Judgment* was hardly worth a worry. "Jaxar," he said, switching his attention back to his engineer, "tell me our shields are ready."

"One hundred percent, warlord," his lead engineer said. The sound of humming electronics filled the background. "We got incoming?"

"Keep those shields up. I don't care if you have to drain

power and every pair of balls on C deck freezes; keep those shields up."

"Understood, sir."

The starfighters turned their attention to the slowing warship, keeping it at a distance and keeping the lead warship harried. Drones deployed and headed towards the disabled ships.

"Sir, the ship is preparing to fire," Zadran said.

"Let them know it's a bad idea to mess with my ship. Fire at will."

"Yes, sir," the male said, firing a wide scattered shot as a warning. Zadran had orders to discourage the Suhlik ship, not destroy. Not yet.

"Rohn, how much time do your drones need?"

"Three minutes. The tractor cable doesn't want to attach. I'm doing it manually."

"Zadran, give him three minutes." Each ship was a life. "Mylomon, tell me you're moments away from disabling that ship."

Static came over the connection. Then, "Trying to decide what button to push. Left or right, warlord."

"Surprise me." Everyone had to be a comedian. Clearly the skirmish was not challenging enough if his men felt they could joke. The next trap needed to have four warships, possibly an entire fleet.

"Incoming fire," Zadran shouted.

A blast hit the shield. The *Judgment* rocked gently, like a boat on a calm ocean.

"Shield report," Paax barked.

"Holding at 90%."

"They seem to have their trigger stuck in the locked position. Incoming," Zadran said.

Another volley hit and the *Judgment* rocked side to side. The lights flickered briefly as Jaxar diverted power.

"75%, sir."

"You seem to think my shields are optional, Jaxar," Paax snarled.

"Working on it, sir."

On the screen, Kleve had the Suhlik captain on the floor with his hand behind his head. Even with his feet and hands tied, the captain opened his mouth and snapped viciously at the warrior. Kleve dodged to the left, narrowly avoiding the Suhlik taking a chunk out of his ear.

"We have the captain's surrender," Jolyon announced.

The lights on the Suhlik ship went dark. Mylomon had finally pressed a button or randomly torn out a chunk of the ship's wiring. Paax didn't care to know the particulars.

"Life support and all power is disabled," Mylomon said.

"Good job. Come on home." He switched his attention to Jolyon. "How many Suhlik do you have in your custody?"

"Enough. A dozen."

"Load them up on a shuttle and launch it to the other Suhlik ship. Let them figure out what to do with a captain that lost his ship to a pack of dogs." The Suhlik captain on the floor thrashed some more before Kleve hit him in the back of the head with the butt of his rifle.

"Sorry, sir. He was agitated and bound to hurt himself."

"Just get them on a shuttle in one piece. How are my shields, Jaxar?"

"Healthy and bouncing like a babe, just don't pick a fight until I repair some conduits."

"Sir, the other ship is retreating," Darian said.

The battle was over. Now it was time for the clean up. Paax went through a mental checklist. "Mylomon, send the raiding parties back once you've rounded up the Suhlik. Rohn, tell me you've salvaged my ships."

"Half are secured," Rohn said.

"Good. I want my starfighters to escort the raiding party back and protect the drones until their work is done."

"Very good, sir."

"Jaxar, when you get my shields repaired, I have a *colpor* for you to play with."

"And I didn't get you anything, sir. I'm flattered."

"Would you be able to make it fly?"

"I won't know until I look at the consol. If those lizards were too busy to set the self-destruct, then yes. I'll get it back to Sangrin for you." The Suhlik were notorious for

NANCEY CUMMINGS & STARR HUNTRESS

setting a self-destruct on their equipment, ships and bases.

"Let's hope we kept them occupied," Paax said. He relaxed into the captain's chair. His warriors could handle the details of the clean up. An hour ago he held his mate, content and at ease; now he waited impatiently for the raiding parties to return. Once those warriors were aboard and the injured sent to medical, he'd be free to seek out his mate.

Antomas remained a problem, as did the male who betrayed their flight plan. Paax suspected Antu leaked information to his brother but Paax would root out the truth. There could be one or more sympathizers, too cowardly to challenge their warlord directly. Their cowardice endangered his mate. For that he would hunt them down and end their pathetic existence. He felt ashamed that he allowed them to linger on the *Judgment*. One does not tolerate a gangrenous limb. It is removed before the sickness spreads.

His thoughts returned back to Antomas. The younger warlord believed himself clever but he was a grasping child, reaching for a prize beyond his capabilities. He was clumsy and brash, and that would get him killed. Paax would see to that but not today.

Today he needed his mate, needed to hold her and listen to the smooth, even beats of her Terran heart.

After an eternity, but really only fifteen minutes, the raiding ships departed one by one until only Mylomon's vessel remained. The Suhlik shuttle launched and drifted away from the ship.

"Casualties?" Paax asked.

"Minimal, sir," Jolyon said.

"I want every scrape and nick examined. No exceptions. If anyone thinks they will tough it out, I will personally see that Kalen Haas wakes them every morning for a full month with an examination." The Suhlik often poisoned their weapons and even their claws. A Mahdfel warrior could receive a shallow cut, think it nothing and be dead within a day. Having daily exams from the head medic was marginally less painful than death by poison.

"Understood."

Finally Mylomon's ship left the Suhlik craft. "Any trouble with the round up?" Paax asked.

"Just the normal insults and shock at being bested by an abomination." So a normal interaction then.

Zadran interrupted, "Sir, the Suhlik vessel is preparing to fire."

"Shields! I want my fighters covering our raiding party now." Paax sprang from his seat. It take a critical hit now, after the battle was over, was an insult but not below those lizards. It was sloppy of him to let his guard down, to assume the conflict over while Suhlik still breathed and had access to weaponry.

"It's turning away from us," Darian said, disbelief coloring his voice.

Paax watched as the Suhlik warship turned on its shuttle

and fired. The shuttle burst into a ball of light then nothing. Typical. The Suhlik never surrendered and refused to accept those who did, even their own.

"You have the bridge," Paax said to Darian. He went to the flight deck to greet the returning raiders. Then, finally, he would find his mate.

Mercy

BRAITH JUMPED to his feet and scurried up the ladder.

Mercy held her breath. It could be Paax sounding the all-clear or it could be a Suhlik at their door.

The hatch opened and a familiar, one-horned visage peered down. She let out her breath in a sigh of relief. "About time," she said with a smile.

"I was waiting for a dramatic entrance. Did that do?"

That impossible male.

CHAPTER 12

Paax

The day of the Naming Ceremony arrived swiftly. Mercy washed and dressed Axil and Drake in overly long white tunics.

"It's a Christening gown."

"Why is there lace?" It hardly seemed practical.

"Because that's traditional."

"Lace."

"The white gown."

"And your parents subjected you to this? I did not know Terrans had a naming ceremony."

"It's called a Christening, actually, and it's similar."

"Will they always have to wear this garment?"

"What? No. It's just for the ceremony." Satisfied that the

boys were fed, washed and dressed, she handed them off to Dorothy.

"I'll watch them while you get ready," she said.

Mercy laid out a pale lavender robe and started to undress. She was breathtakingly lovely as she disrobed. He watched her go through these motions a hundred times and never grew tired of the sight.

Paax took her hands and drew her away. "I have to get dressed," she said.

"Let me wash you, little star."

"We don't have time—"

His kiss silenced her protest. She grew soft against him. "The ceremony waits for us. There is no rush."

"I'm feeling a little under dressed here."

He disrobed immediately, standing firm for her inspection. Her fingers skated across the scar on his shoulder. "I didn't know you were injured."

"It is nothing."

Her eyes flashed. "We've had this conversation. That's not nothing."

He took her hand and brought her fingertips to his lips. "I was injured. I healed. Do not worry."

Her pupils went wide and her nipples hardened. The musky scent of her arousal perfumed the air and he hardened in response. He pressed her to him, grinding his cock against her stomach. "See what you do to me, little star."

Her hand drifted down and wrapped around his cock. He groaned at her touch. She stroked the length of him.

He pulled away and knelt at her feet. Confusion filled her eyes. "Today is about you, mate. Not me. Let me serve you. Let me pleasure you."

Gently, he pressed his lips to his mate's still soft and round belly. Red marks appeared vivid against her pale skin. She was beautiful, creation and life in soft, resilient vessel. "A miracle happened here," he murmured.

Mercy

PAAX LED her into the cleansing room and stood with her under the streaming water. Gently he worked shampoo into her hair, massaging her scalp with his strong fingers, careful to keep suds out of her eyes. He finger-combed her long hair, working the conditioner in. He worked soap into a thick lather on her body. Using his hand, he scooped water and rinsed away the lather one scoop at a time.

Everywhere he touched ached for him, for more. His hands massaged down her arms, across her back and shoulders and tenderly worked the sensitive flesh of her breasts. Heavy and aching, she craved his mouth on her.

"Paax—"

"Hush. I'm not done worshiping you."

He knelt at her feet, hands working a lather across her belly, her hips and bottom. His hands glided down her thighs and then skimmed up the inside. Unconsciously she widened her stance for him.

He leaned in to the apex of her thighs and breathed in, like she was the greatest thing he ever smelled. His dark lashes rested on the warm plum of his skin, fluttering. An aching hollow feeling flared deep within her. She needed him as much as he clearly desired her.

"Paax, I want you but I'm not ready." Not for him to plunge deep within her, as much as she craved him to fill her.

He made a placating, soothing noise, the vibrations going to straight to her core. Her hips rocked forward, eager. One hand hooked behind her leg and lifted it over his shoulder, resting it there.

His mouth sought out her pussy, tongue diving into her folds. One hand remained on her bottom, keeping her in place, not that she was about to go anywhere. He lapped at her, savoring all of her. His tongue, rough and wet, circled her clit. The sensation was enough to drive her over the edge but he pressed on. His lips clamped over her and sucked.

Mercy looked down and saw his hard, thick cock in hand, stroking. The tattoos across his shoulders, chest and back cast a silvery light.

He was speaking to her but she couldn't focus. She caught

fragments of words like "mine" and "best". Her husband was the best but that probably wasn't what he was saying.

She placed one hand on his head for stability and the other grabbed him by the horn to steer. This pushed his wonderful mouth into overdrive. Pressure and speed increased like he was a man starved. They both were. It seemed so long since they had a moment to themselves, to enjoy themselves, without the discomfort of a pregnant belly. Though, honestly, Paax didn't seem to mind at the time. Quite the opposite, in fact.

His tongue speared her entrance, sending her over. Her knees trembled and her grip tightened on his horn. She nearly slipped down but he held her up, letting her hips buck as she rode out her climax.

Paax pressed the side of his cheek against her belly, his horn dangerously close to her nipples. She watched as his hand worked his length, fast and tight with a twist at the head. He released, splashing his hot seed against her thigh and sagged against her.

"I love you with every fiber of my being. The moment I saw you, I knew I belonged to you. You make my heart whole," he said.

Her fingers worked through his wet hair. He smiled up at her, vivid blue eyes shining. Whatever the future held, she knew that he was her home and her family.

CHAPTER 13

Mercy

The ceremonial robe was far more complex than she anticipated. Paax helped her navigate the long sleeves that draped over her hands and then fasten the thick belt. Satisfied that every fold laid correctly, he presented her with a beaded necklace. A crystal and amethyst star pendant hung in the center, surrounded by multi-color glass beads. For the last two weeks, warriors had been giving her the beads with the utmost seriousness. She accepted them graciously but put the beads in a bowl, not knowing what to do with them. Somehow Paax strung the beads into a necklace.

Even with the chain long enough to wrap around her neck twice, the pendant still hung down her chest.

"When did you have time to make this?" she asked, marveling at the fine chain.

"How many times do I have to tell you that there is nothing I will not do for you, little star?"

The sweetest things. Honestly.

In the arena, the sight and sound of the entire *Judgment* clan overwhelmed her. A thousand feet stomped. A thousand warriors cheered.

They cheered for her.

The infant in her arms shifted and fussed. Axil didn't like the noise. She bounced him and cooed.

Paax beamed, carrying a fussing Drake.

He led her to the center platform. There was no podium, no water basin or other prop. It was just their family on display. She felt the weight of all those warrior eyes on her.

A male approached, older with silver shot through his dark hair and his horn an iron grey. He held a cylindrical device in his hands. He bowed and held out the device for Paax's inspection. This must be the tattoo artist.

He nodded. The male joined them on the platform.

The crowd fell silent.

Mercy scanned the audience. Within the last year, she had met or spoken to most of these warriors. She went out of her way to greet all the females. She knew only a handful well, only a dozen or so names, but they all knew her.

Stage fright did not begin to cover the emotions within her.

Paax leaned and pressed his lips to her ear. "The naming ceremony is not complicated. Normally it is for family only and is private."

"But since you're the warlord—"

"Yes. The clan demands a spectacle. It will be over fast."

She nodded. She could handle fast.

"Female," Paax said in a loud, booming voice. She recognized it as his *warlord* voice, the one with unquestionable authority. "You have given me a treasure beyond compare. What do I call this warrior?"

Mercy peered down at Drake, face flush and dusky pink. His complexion grew more like Paax's every day but reverted to pink when he cried. His bright blue eyes were screwed closed and his mouth opened, emitting a passionate wail.

Of course Axil had to join his brother. They were a team that way.

"Drake Nawk," she said, placing a kiss on the crying babe's head. He calmed at his mother's touch.

The male pressed the barrel of the device to the infant's chest. Mercy held her breathe. Paax said the tattoo wouldn't hurt but he wasn't above a fib…

A brief flare of light and it was done. The male removed the device and revealed a spiral tattoo, no bigger than a coin. Drake's crying remained the same, unaffected by the tattoo. It glowed, silvery against dusky skin.

"Drake!" Paax lifted him high, presenting him to the clan.

The crowd erupted in cheers, drowning out Drake's cries.

When the crowd stilled, Paax turned back to Mercy. They exchanged their bundles with practiced efficiency.

"Female, my star and mate, you have given me yet another treasure. I am unworthy of your consideration."

Mercy smirked. "Yes you are," she whispered, only for his ears.

"What do I call this warrior?"

She kissed Axil's head. "Axil Nawk."

The scene repeated, both infants crying with displeasure. Their cries only seemed to amuse the warriors in the crowd. She caught shouts of "strong lungs" and "fierce battle cry." Mahdfel priorities, she guessed.

The crowd filtered by them, each one stopping to greet them, murmur admiration and knock horns with Paax. Axil and Drake liked this much better, gurgling and displaying how good they were at shoving feet into their mouths. This was their family and their place in the universe. A year ago she could not imagine such happiness. While their marriage was far from perfect, it was good. Solid. Time would only make them stronger. They might disagree with each other occasionally but they always loved each other.

This was her place in the universe.

She loved the person standing with her.

She glowed with joy.

EPILOGUE

Seeran

Seeran took to running on the beach. The uneven surface with variable wet and dry texture proved an interesting challenge and worked the muscles in his lower legs in a way hard surface running did not. He ran at dawn just as the Terran sun rose over the ocean's edge, turning the water into liquid gold. He ran at noon with the dual punishment of the hot sun beating down and reflecting off the water. He ran at dusk, as shadows spread and obfuscated any obstacles in the sand.

It's not like he had anything better to do. Seeran was stuck on Earth until Vox and his mate finished their business. Vox protested and claimed he could protect his mate without Seeran's assistance but Seeran had a direct order from the warlord to safeguard the pilot's female until she returned to the *Judgment*. So he remained on Earth, bored. Vox seemed happy enough to gobble down Terran food and watch unending entertainment programs. Pilots, it seemed, were familiar with long periods of idle waiting before a sudden scramble to action.

Seeran, however, was not used to being idle. The inactivity got under his skin, to borrow the Terran phrase, and itched, demanding release. There were only so many times he could patrol the perimeter, observing the same Terrans walk their odd four-legged companion animals at the same time every day, before he went stir-crazy.

Cabin fever, Carrie called it.

So he ran. Fast. Hard. As often as possible until the excess energy left his body.

On the beach, there were new sights and sounds, new targets to evaluate and assign a threat level.

The sun overhead created a pleasant warmth on his bare skin. Terrans claimed small parcels of the beach and lounged on their respective flags. So strange. Their territorial claims were temporary and they would release their beachfront domains when the sun sat in the west. Each day, he observed this behavior but could not make sense of it. Each new day brought new territorial claims, erasing the previous day like so much shifting sand. At least the Terran made for interesting obstacles and the younger ones tried to run with him. Seeran would slow his pace, to let their short legs keep the pace. Running slower on the sand required more effort, so he did not mind.

Over the sea air, the salt, and the chemical odor of sunscreen, an aroma caught Seeran's attention. It was hard to describe, like the flowers that bloomed at night in his mother's garden but also green and warm, distinctly Terran, and, more importantly, his.

His mate.

His route took him toward the heady aroma, toward a cluster of Terrans lounging on their territorial flags, soaking in the sun's radiation. There were several females in the crowd, all wearing bathing costumes that covered little and exposed much. His eyes scanned over them, none of them seemed particularly interesting.

One female stood out. She argued with a male, tugging on the flag used to claim a plot of the sand. Her face flushed red, not from sun exposure but from upset. The male loomed over her, trying to cow her with physical intimidation.

"I'm not leaving until you cover up. I can't let you walk around like a whore, Hazel. I won't let people talk about my woman that way."

"Fine. If you won't leave," she said, dropping the flag, "I will."

"Don't you walk away from me," the male said, grabbing her wrist and pulling her towards him. His fingers dug into her flesh, leaving white imprints. The male was hurting this female.

Seeran's female.

Hazel.

In a heartbeat, Seeran was between the male and his female. He grabbed the male's arm and twisted just so, forcing him to release the female. "What do you think you're doing, you purple idiot?" the male asked, surprise on his face.

Seeran snorted. He was magenta, not purple. This male was blind as well as foolish. "It is unlawful to detain a person against their will," he said.

"Listen, I appreciate everything your people did in the war and all, but this is between me and my wife."

His wife. Hazel already had a mate. Seeran's heart sank.

THANK YOU FOR READING!

I HOPE you enjoyed revisiting Paax and Mercy and the babies. Sometimes it's a bit odd for a writer to have two people continue to live their lives in the back of your head. The adventure continues with Seeran and, yes, Antomas will get his comeuppance. Paax is not one for hollow promises.

TYPOS ARE sneaky beasts and they slip past both my editor and proofreader. If you found one or a formatting error, please me an email at Nancey@menurapress.com and I'll get right on it.

ABOUT THE AUTHOR

Join my newsletter and get a FREE copy of Claimed by the Alien Prince.

Get it at here:

https://dl.bookfunnel.com/jektemqay4

I write fun, flirty and fast stories featuring sassy heroines, out-of-this-world heroes, all

the mischief they can managed and plenty of steamy fun. Hopefully you want to read

them too.

I live in an old house with my husband and a growing collection of cats.

Follow my Facebook reader group for early teasers and whatnots.

https://www.facebook.com/groups/895051017325998/

ALSO BY NANCEY CUMMINGS

Tail and Claw (Celestial Mates)

Have Tail, Will Travel

Pulled by the Tail

Valos of Sonhadra

Blazing

Inferno

Taken for Granite (Khargals of Duras)

Dragons of Wye (with Juno Wells)

Korven's Fire

Ragnar

Alpha Aliens of Fremm

Claimed by the Aline Prince

Bride of the Alien Prince

Alien Warrior's Mate

Alien Rogue's Price

CPSIA information can be obtained
at www.ICGtesting.com
Printed in the USA
LVHW112312041119
636249LV00006B/466/P